THE REJECTED WORKS

Volume I

short stories

WILLIAM L. DOMME

These short stories were written by William L. Domme.

Copyright © 2013 William L. Domme. All rights reserved. No part of this book may be used or reproduced in any manner whatsoever without written permission except in the case of brief quotations embodied in critical articles and reviews.

The High Price originally appeared in the Spring 2013 issue of The Subterranean Quarterly.

Cover design contains a painting by Kansas based artist Matthew Miller who graciously allowed its use.

First Edition published 2013

Domme, William L. (1979-)
    The Rejected Works Volume I
    ISBN 978-1-300-94260-3

More stories and information available here: **atypeofwriter.com**

The Rejected Works
Volume I

William L. Domme

The Dogshit Summer
Idler at the Window
Knuckles' Broken Promise
Malcolm's Apple Tree
Morning
Stellan Bambrey
Talk of Sex Over Wine: Wrong Place, Wrong Time
The High Price
They Oughtta Make a Law
From a Hand You've Once Shaken
The Snake in the Hourglass
The Death of Marcus Kasparov
The News on TV

THE DOGSHIT SUMMER

The phone is loud, the kids are screaming at each other, and the throbbing in my head must be the first step on a short trip to an aneurysm. My eyes are trying to escape my head because they can't convince the lids to close and the fingers trying to button the bottom button on my shirt play some weird game of tag that keeps me from getting on with the day.

The car shakes so bad when I put the brakes on at every stop that the steering wheel rocks side to side and almost rips itself out of my hands. It's hard to concentrate on the road with this and the kids playing as we go to Fannie's, their sitter, before I have to work.

The streets are already hot and ugly at ten in the morning. No clouds. No shade. Even the trees seem to be packing up for a different climate. Shelby's in the backseat trying to fog over the window with her breath and even though there's no fog, pulls her finger across the glass, "What are you drawing baby?"

"That dog on the side of the road."

"Where?"

"Back there."

"That dog was dead," Hank Jr. says.

"No he wasn't," Shelby slaps at him and misses, "Mommy, can we get a puppy?"

"We'll see."

The surface of everything looks bad, the whole town, single story buildings put up through a dozen decades, with their different styles and fashions, look like empty shells painted over, starting to blister and crack, ready to flake away and float into the wind like the soft white bulbs from the cottonwood trees that drift along; making it look like snow in the heart of the summer. A moment of dreaming makes me think the window of my door is liquefying and running down on itself.

It's back to work, for me, for a half shift at Harold's Steak & Brew. The past week was the disaster of my life and the months leading up to it, the years really, screamed at the impending doom. I don't throw that word out there lightly. There would be death, prison, and failure but seriously, how was I to know? I have three kids to raise and had a husband to baby-sit. There was no time to look at the signs.

* * *

Our trailer vibrates with a rattle, again. I just want to read the new Harlequin book. It was the Harlequin/NASCAR series of books I'd found at Wal-Mart last winter when we were looking for a heavy winter coat for Hank to wear to work. That was when he was working for the garbage company. He lost that job because of a urine test. Shit.

The neighbor's stereo is blaring and the bass is shaking every house in the neighborhood. I've told Carl James about this before but I guess he doesn't know that I'm home today. Hank's collection of beer cans dances on the shelf above the plasma TV. They're empty so they get to moving pretty good.

Hank Jr., Shelby, and Cody are down at Hank's parents' house just down the street a ways where the trailer park lowers to a pretty wooded park type area. On the other side of Stranger's Crick, the stream that runs down to the river, is the women's prison.

I had the house to myself, except for the noise. Hank is supposedly down at the crick, fishing with a friend he hasn't heard from since high school but I guess it's only three years ago that Hank dropped out of junior year.

Feeling the book rest on my thigh but unable to come out of it, like my whole body is asleep except my mind, I decide to look for Hank's pot. It should be in the nylon bag where his Glock is supposed to go but from the couch I can see the gun on top of the refrigerator. The book falls to the couch and I walk to the bedroom.

The room's a mess but I know where everything is pretty much. The bag is under a pile of damp clothes next to our bed. Looks to be just enough for a skinny joint and that should do the trick. I haven't smoked up to now since when I found out I was preggo, bout nineteen months ago. Wow, I realize Cody's near to a year old. I'm only twenty-one.

"Papers. Papers? Papers?" I sing while I riffle through the pot accessories on the dresser. "There you are."

Back on the couch, trying to get comfortable, stretching and throwing the kids' clothes they'd left lying around, I get upset they aren't picking up after themselves. Laying down, about ready to light up, the smell of flat sody and stale bourbon blows at me from the half full cups on the table poured at the end of the party here Sunday night. Must be some cigarette butts in there too cause I smell 'em also. For a minute I'm sixteen again cleaning out the men's room at Harold's, scrubbing out the urinals, dragging soggy butts up the rim and into the bucket on the floor using the little scrubby brush. Not caring cause all I could think about was getting off work, sitting out with Hank at Stranger's Crick, getting high, and fucking like animals.

The window unit a.c. blows cold air across the house and makes the paper burn faster than the weed in the joint. The better part of it is almost lost so I turn to face the back of the couch and shield it against the rushing air. It clicks off and I roll onto my back again. A piece of the cherry falls to the couch and smolders a little hole into the cushion. I put it out with the leg of a pair of Hank's jeans.

Laying down, holding the joint in one hand and the book in the other, the smoke fills the room. I'm getting high again for the first time in two years. It's my day off and the closest I'll get to a real vacation.

I must have passed out cause I wake up and hear the bass from a car parked just outside the door. Getting up to go to the door I knock over one of the stale cups on the table and have to sop up the poison brew with the pair of Hank's pants I used to put out the couch. The door slams against the outside of the house and I stare out into the white heat unable to see for a couple of minutes cause my eyelids feel stuck together and my lips appear to be glued shut also. Damn cottonmouth.

I hear, "Hey sweet tits, you're up."

"You're out of pot." I shut the door and hear him cuss me to Tyler Ferry. They're back from fishing. I'm at the sink doing some dishes looking out the little window and see the two of them standing around Tyler's car, I guess, with a Styrofoam cooler on the hood, a big chunk broken off the corner and sitting in the grass. They drink tall boys and I see Shelby hitting the barbeque-er with a branch bigger than her arm. Carl James comes out of his trailer and walks over to the guys. I prick my finger with a knife I'm scrubbing, say, "Fucking Carl James," cause it's his fault I'm scrubbing mad now. He's a no-good low life and keeps Hank from getting a real job. Lets Hank help him sell small amounts of meth and pot and recycle copper wire. Pretty sure Carl James just siphons gas from cars at the mall instead of going to a gas station. Gets drunk, calls it his own personal gas station.

Shelby comes into the house, "Mommy."

"Bay-bee."

"Mommy, I'm going back to Granma's."

"Have your daddy walk you down there."

"Bye mommy."

"Bye," the door bangs shut, "baby." I scrub harder at a dish.

She tells Hank. He waves her on down. Just stands there drinking with Carl, James and Tyler. Tyler, at least raises an eyebrow. I stop with the dishes and look in the fridge for something to eat.

The front door squeaks open like some giant dinosaur bird tearing at the metal roof of the house. Popping up to see who's coming in I bump my head on the door handle of the freezer. "Shit." I mumble.

Hank is carrying a plastic sack full of clunky metal and wires that stick through like rosebush clippings in a plastic lawn bag. It looks like another stolen stereo. He clenches a cigarette between his straight, white teeth saying, "Welcome home baby, I made dinner," and throws the sack on the couch.

"When you come home from a day at work I'll make you dinner."

"I'm looking for work."

"Where, in other people's cars?"

"What are we going to do about that kid?"

"What kid?"

"Hank Jr. They were all set to play at Mom and Dad's, I told him he could swim as long as he wanted and out of nowhere he starts fittin' like he was a daughter and not my son and crying for me to take him with me. So, he's been with me the whole day." He pulls down the Glock from the top of the fridge and checks the chamber and then the clip. The slamming of the metal parts echoes in the trailer.

"So what's in the sack on the couch?"

"You hear me? I'm saying our son's acting like a little sissy and you wanna know what's in the bag? It's a fucking CB radio."

"What are you, Smokey and The Bandit now? What the hell we gonna do with a cb? And whose money did you spend on it?"

"Didn't spend nobody's money on it. Wheelin' Tom owed me for a couple of grams and we picked it up on our way back."

"So this is your business, trading meth for obsolete communications devices?"

"You high again?" He grabs my face by the cheeks and turns my head side to side looking into my eyes. "You only talk like that when you used to smoke."

"Told you, you were out of pot."

"Thought you were quitting?" he says, walking over to the front door. "Course, see your smut book open there."

"What about your dvd collection?"

"Our dvd collection. What happen, you start getting all sweaty," he walks toward me in slow stalking steps, "reading about them racers, so you toked a little and started fantasizing?" Coupons and magnets fall off the fridge when I back into it. They flutter and crash to the torn up linoleum floor. He pins me right there. Finishes. And I finish the dishes.

Saturday night at Harold's Steak & Brew is the busiest night of the week. "It's like bleaching sheets in a madhouse." Polly says. She's drying bar glasses while I pour drinks for the waiters and waitresses. Most of them are still in high school and think their job isn't permanent. The ones who don't escape become the bartenders and cooks and hostesses. I mix up four Tom Collins' for a table of Realtors who come in every other Saturday. Two nice couples, tip big, leave drunk.

"Sorry, what?" I say.

"Bleaching sheets in a madhouse?" Polly's bending over dropping glasses in soapy water in the big steel sink behind the bar. "They're usually all decked out in white. So…"

"Oh. I see. Nice metaphor." My face twitches.

"You got it."

"Go in the back and get me two bottles of Jack Daniel's, Polly."

"Two Seven & Seven's, one Jack & Coke, and three Bud Lights." Missy says blowing the bangs up off her forehead.

"Crazy night." I look at her for a moment. We used to be friends.

"Yep," she turns around to look over the tables.

Victor comes rushing up to the bar, he's a waiter, in Polly's class at the same high school. "Hey, can I get four cokes?"

"You can come back here and pour them. It'll be faster." Before I get the sentence out of my mouth he's around the edge of the bar. He's a worker.

"You know Polly's up for valedictorian?" He says. "It's a tie right now." He's practically out of breath and I think it's because he wants to get into Polly's pretty little panties; she's a good-looking girl. He starts putting the cokes on the tray. "She'll probably get it though cause she volunteers and all that other stuff."

"Slow down, Victor. Those cokes will be on the floor if you don't breathe," Missy says.

Polly comes back with the two bottles of Jack. "Where do you want them?"

"Up here, we'll pour them before the night's over with," I say.

"Jeez, that's a lot of booze."

"Not really. You should see Hank put that shit away."

She raises her eyes. "So, last months of high school."

"You know where you're going? Probably Washburn?"

"No, I think I could get into a better school. I don't know."

I feel stupid and my face feels warmer. She furrows her brow and seems ashamed of her statement.

"So where are you thinking about?"

"I sent applications and stuff to Middlebury and Coe College." She looks to see if they sound familiar, I think. "Coe is in Cedar Rapids, Iowa and Middlebury is in Middlebury, Vermont."

"Quite a stretch. How'd you find those?"

"I looked up the colleges of two of my favorite writers who are still alive."

"So, you want to be writer?"

"No way. I just want to study literature. But I thought it would be cool to walk where they walked." Harold is glad-handing with the patrons and keeps looking back to see what we're doing at the bar. He leers like I'm not wearing clothes and I get a little nauseous.

He made a pass at me two years ago in the kitchen after work and I thought about saying yes to him for a good minute or two before remembering that Ian had told me

Harold had the clap. Now, I throw up in my mouth a little every time I remember that moment.

* * *

The night winds down to the last table.

"Harold's in his office." Polly says.

"He'll be in there until we finish cleaning up. He never comes out until it's time for all of us to leave."

"Doesn't like to clean up?"

"Likes to watch on the video cameras. Try not to bend over too much."

"Gross." She wrinkles her face up and it looks like it hurts.

My cigarette burns slow in the glass ashtray at the end of the bar and I catch Polly looking at it every time she gets near it. Finally, "Do you want one?"

"No, they remind me of my father," she says. "He…"

"I know. So, I've been thinking about going to Washburn and taking classes to get a degree. Even just an associates."

"I said you should. You can get a better job than this one."

"You probably know more than me about getting in. Do you think you could help me with it?"

"You want to meet me at the library and we can fill out the application, like on Sunday?"

My heart races at the thought of going to college; all the people, the tests, the homework. "Okay. Two okay?"

"See you there."

The bag of food on the seat next to me makes the car smell like the exhaust fan above the grill at Harold's. I think I'll never get away from that place. The thought of going to school again makes me feel excited though, almost to a panic.

Pulling into the trailer park I imagine for a second that it's a neighborhood with actual houses. Then the cars in front of our house remind me of where I live. Hank's having a party. A group from the restaurant are here, always are when there's a party. I can hear the music before I open the car door and I breathe out for a minute.

A few people are standing on the little wooden steps that go up to the front door, smoking and drinking and slapping each other on the arm. They separate for me so I can get in the door and there's Hank; standing on the couch getting ready to jump down on Ian, the cook. They're doing their wrestling show again for everybody. The house is packed. "Food," he yells at me and jumps on Ian who turned to look. Hank gets up and walks up to me to grab the sack. "What do you got?"

"Mushrooms…"

"Shroooooms," he yells.

The crowd mutters about shrooms and it gets the different groups standing around talking about the times they've tripped on mushrooms. "Mushrooms, fries and gravy, and a chicken fried steak," I tell him.

He kisses me on the cheek and tears the bag out of my hand and takes it to the kitchen counter. He's washing big bites of food down with huge gulps of whatever he's drinking. The whole house smells like cigarettes and booze. The stink of grease and meat sneaks up my nose though and I go back to the bedroom to change. The party lasts for hours.

Until the last of the drinkers are left. That's when the political talk starts. And the religious arguments bulge and pop in booze pickled hiccups. And everyone left agrees they love each other and would kill and die for each other and then the last of them get to their cars to swerve and blur their cars like fuzzy stripes through the empty streets at four in the morning.

I fall asleep just before the sun comes up. It's hot as shit as I lay there on top of the sheet that hasn't been washed for a month. It smells like alcohol and cigarettes and burned plastic because that is how Hank smells a lot of the time.

He doesn't get to bed before he passes out on a bar stool in the kitchen surrounded by half full cups that serve as ashtrays and spittoons. This is how I find him around eleven in the morning.

He begins to rustle around as I get my clothes on and pick up a little. "What time is it?" he says.

"Almost noon," I pause, "on Monday."

"No way."

"Sunday. I'm going down to your folks to get the kids. You want to take a shower?"

"I'm good."

"You want to take a shower. You smell like you been sleeping in pig shit."

"Alright, mama."

"See you in a minute."

*   *   *

Outside the sun is burning hard. The smell of dog shit hangs over the yard. And then I see the culprits; Carl James' two giant boxers penned up outside his trailer. They just mope and prowl, sniffing the gravel and each other, and biting flies off their own backs, coughing out air like a couple of old men smoking at a bar. Carl James is passed out on his back, legs hanging off the back of his white Dodge pick-up. The steel from the tailgate has to be burning like a cattle brand into his calves. Hope it burns them right off. I spit out a couple of sunflower seeds in his direction and walk around and down the road to Hank's folks'.

The kids look like angels. They're laid back on the couch watching a movie. Vera and Lou play cards at a little table between the couch and kitchen. They all say hey mom, even Lou and Vera. "Watcha watching?"

"Cars," Shelby says and goes back to watching with her eyes barely open. The paper is laid out on the table where I sit for a minute.

"Well, how was the party?" Lou says. "Gin."

"Again he wins."

"You've been winning all morning."

"What's news?" I thumbed through the papers but didn't really read anything.

"Bobbo was killed last night."

"What?" I look at Lou waiting for this to mean something.

"He was shot outside the Muddy Creek Saloon. They know who did it but they ain't caught him yet," Lou says and drinks his orange juice.

"Her, they ain't caught her yet," Vera says.

"Her?"

"They gave her name in the paper, bottom of the front page." Vera says. Cody starts to turn in the little crib next to the table. He sleeps some more. Flipping the paper to the front I see the name before I set it down.

"No shit. Claire Hibbert." My eyes go all buggy and then settle back down.

"That's not the Claire from your high school?" Lou says.

"Yeah, she beat the crap out of a lot of girls in health class when it was time to take showers. Big girl. Mean girl."

"You ask me, Bobbo should've have got the death penalty for what happened to Terri Crensh." Lou drinks his orange juice again, empty, he gets up to get some more from the fridge. "That guy crawls through the cab window of a truck while it's being driven. The gun in his hand, he thinks isn't 'loaded', goes off and kills poor Terri and he doesn't get convicted of even negligent homicide. Screw that guy." He sits back down at the table and shuffles the cards.

"Forgot about that. What a scumbucket. He went to Terri's funeral with his new girlfriend. Him and Terri were together for a year almost."

"She shouldn't have been hanging out with that crowd in the first place. Big Bobbo did time for assaulting a police officer when Little Bobbo was five. He got pulled over for speeding and wasn't having it and just started wailing on the cop." Vera spreads the cards she was dealt in her hand.

Lou lights a cigarette and it fills the air that up to now smelled like cinnamon rolls.

"Well we better get out of your hair. Let you guys have the rest of your day."

"Just going to Wal-Mart to stock up on a few necessities." Vera lays down a card.

* * *

A couple of bees float up and down by Shelby's arm as we walk to the house. Hank Jr. takes a step and plants each foot and pauses to watch the dust kick up and drift behind him. "Cool," he walks this way all the way up the road. I don't tell Shelby about the bee cause it might freak her out. Cody's shirt smells cleaner than when I put it in his bag yesterday before I dropped them off.

"Hey kids." Hank folds laundry that's separated across the couch. "Want to help daddy fold the clothes?" To my surprise Hank Jr. says yes and he and his sister go over to help Hank with the pile of laundry tangled up on the end of the couch.

"What happened to you?" I said.

"Nothing baby, you were down for so long I had time to clean a little and get the laundry going," Hank said.

The place looks…clean. It still smells faintly of last night's drinking but more of lemon scented cleaners and soap. "Thanks baby." I kiss him on the neck, he smells like soap, shampoo, and cologne and I'm surprised. The water is running from the tap while I look for a cup in the cupboard.

"I made tea too, it's in the fridge." Hank doesn't look up from the laundry. I think he must have taken a bump when I woke him up earlier. He'll do a bump and then do fifty productive things out of the blue.

"Kids want anything to drink?"

"Pepsi," they say together.

They grab the cans of pop out of my hands and start getting antsy right away. "Can we light the rest of the snakes? Can we? Can we?"

"Sure kids, go get them."

They run to the bedroom behind the wall the TV's on and rip through a plastic sack full of little fireworks leftover from the fourth. The door slams and I can hear Hank Jr. jump down the wooden steps and crunch across the gravel. Hank goes to the door, "Keep 'em out of the grill."

"Wow," I said.

"What?"

"Been busy. Tweakin?"

"All tweakend long. Get's the job done." He laughs and his shoulders and head bounce in opposite directions. He's a fucking bobblehead.

A sigh slips out and he gets offended so he goes out to watch the kids burn the snakes. He makes sure to pick up a tall boy on the way out the door.

"Christ." I walk to the bedroom and sit down for a minute. The Glock is on the dresser and the clip is sitting next to it. Next to all that is a line of Go-Go. I want to scrape it into a bag and flush it down the toilet. I want to go to college and get a better job, get a better life. Bending over it and sniffing it up my nose with a little straw I start to feel electrified. I pick up the empty gun and toss it between my hands like I'm in the old west, "Annie Oakley rides again." In the mirror on the dresser it all looks cool and then I see the clock on the table behind me. "Shit. The library. Polly."

"Hank." The smell of the burning snakes is in the air along with the dog shit and fresh mowed grass.

"Yeah babe?"

"I-gotta-meet-Polly-at-the-library-at-two. I forgot."

"So go."

"You watch the kids?"

"That's what I'm doing."

My face feels like it isn't there while I wash it with a soap that has little beads in it to exfoliate. Same with my teeth when I brush them. I might be able to clean the ripping buzz off me if I scrub hard enough and then Polly won't see me for who I really am.

The place is packed. Who comes here on Sunday? So many kids and parents walking around the parking lot; everyone looks lost and I definitely want to pull out and go back home. "You gotta do this." In the rearview mirror I look okay, my eyes look clear.

The inside of the library is cold as shit. Not remembering where we were going to meet I just sit on a bench inside the front doors. A lady walks by with a half dozen books in her arms. "Excuse me," I say and she turns to me, "could you tell me what time it is?"

She looks at me like I asked her for a cup of urine. "It's only one now."

"Thanks." And sitting there I can't tell if I'm grinding my teeth because I'm freezing or from the Go-Go. I try to flip through my purse to keep my mind busy but there's nothing to organize and I close it. The automatic doors slide open and Polly walks in. Thank god.

"Hey, I was going to look around before you got here but you're here early too." Polly says. "I gotta put these on the return conveyor." She starts to walk that way.

"Yeah, I haven't been here in a while so I was going to look around but then didn't think we had said where to meet so I thought I'd wait. It's freezing in here, isn't it?"

She walks deep into the library past information desks and tables with computers.

"We'll go back to the quiet room and get online. Should be able to submit the app. through Washburn's site."

"Glad you're here. I wouldn't know the first thing about this."

Twenty minutes later we're out on the sidewalk and she asks me what I'm doing for the rest of the day. The sun is white and bounces off the concrete walls of the library and I can barely see her face that just looks like a shadow in front of me while other shadows walk behind her.

* * *

Bonnie Dick pulls out of the yard when I get home. Inside, Hank is sitting in his shorts with no shirt on playing Xbox. "What's going on?"

"Nothing. Bonnie stopped by with her kid and wanted to know if the kids wanted to go to the pool with them."

"What about Cody?"

"He went with mom and dad to Wal-Marts. Got the casa to ourselves again," Hank says, probably expecting sex.

"Guess I'll see the kids later in the week when I'm done with work."

"Sorry baby, they wanted to go swimming and mom wanted to get Cody some new clothes."

"She suck your dick while she was here?"

"Whoa. What?"

"Sorry, but she's a whore."

"That was in high school."

"Anyway. I applied to Washburn today. Polly helped me."

"How are you going to go to work and school?"

"I was hoping with the student loans I could work part time and then you could look a little harder for a job. I mean you're really good at Call of Duty but how much money have you made killing fake armies?"

"Why don't I sign up for the marines?"

"I don't know, why not?"

"I tried man, they found crank in my blood at the fitness exam. I was clean for almost a month before I went to that."

"So."

He gets up and tosses the controller at the console and grabs a tallboy from the fridge and walks outside. The music from the video game plays until I turn the tube off. Back in the bedroom I fall onto the bed and stare up at the ceiling and imagine what the first day of classes will be like. How will I wear my hair? What clothes do you wear to a college class? Will I be able to stay awake in the classrooms?

I can't sleep but I need a nap. The laundry in the bedroom is piled up as high as the bed and all the way around it. We don't have much laundry soap but I thin it out with water and try to do as much laundry as I can while the kids are gone. Hank must be at Carl James', I don't see him outside anywhere when I pass by the window over the sink. Carl James' truck is gone too, so who knows where they are.

* * *

The door opens about one in the morning. Hank bumps around the living room and I listen, hoping he doesn't wake up the kids but he probably will. Cody's asleep on the bed next to me, he looks like a little turtle with the blanket over his back, his butt stuck up in the air. Hank stands in the doorway bobbing back and forth a little. I whisper, "Cody's asleep on the bed."

"What are you doing sleeping with another man?" he laughs.

"Ha ha. Go to sleep. I've got to work tomorrow. Today, now."

The bed bounces when he rolls into it and Cody shifts around but doesn't wake. I stare up at the ceiling hoping to god that something gets better but I can't say what.

Rain starts to fall and Hank snores.

* * *

Nick pulls into the parking lot at Harold's while I smoke a cigarette and stare at the cornfield across the old highway. My eyes blink slowly while I try to imagine him not here. I'd slept with him one night at the house, when Hank Jr. was just a toddler. Hank was on a canoe trip with Carl James and a few of their buddies down to Oklahoma. I was already pregnant with Shelby but Hank and Nick didn't know. When they did know a couple of months later it caused all kinds of problems. Nick knew if Hank ever found out about the affair and thought Shelby wasn't his he'd kill Nick, no hesitation. I believed it too. Finally, I had to set Nick down and tell him to do the math, that it couldn't be his and that I was pregnant and didn't want to deal with him being so dramatic around me.

Nick gets out of his car. "Yo, baby."

"Nick."

"Whatchoo and Hank up to Friday night?"

"Hank's probably drinking, wouldn't you guess?"

"Thought I'd let you know me and Heather are having a party at our place out on Forty Third Street. You guys should come."

Heather, a trampy little senior who works with us. She hates getting stoned but does it anyway cause she thinks bloodshot eyes make her irresistible to Nick and every other dude at the restaurant. But I think only Wally, the fifty some year old dishwasher, thinks, the two seconds a night she speaks to him, they're in love.

"I'm sure we'll be out there. Hank definitely, but I may stay home with the kids." The gravel crunches under my foot when I step out the butt. Don't ask how Shelby is, you creepy fuck, I think to myself.

"How are the kids?"

"Kids, ya know."

He walks inside and I fake like I forgot something in my car.

Now with the flies. There is a drain in the floor beneath the bar where I spend nine hours a day, six days a week serving gin fizz, cognac, and brandy spritzers to golf course wives who act like they're stepping down to eat in this place. But they come out with their husbands cause it's where their husbands' parents brought them on Sundays when they were teenagers.

The wives talk about shopping trips to Kansas City's Plaza, skiing in Colorada, and the kids away at space camp somewhere in 'Bama. They look at me like I'm not good enough to pour their drinks. A fly scratches my leg as it buzzes around the floor. The wives pass by on their way, stumbling to the toilet, giving advice like, 'don't get tied down to one man' or 'life is short, don't waste it with a dick.'

I imagine them all sneaking off to fake salon appointments to meet up with each other for scandalous lesbian group cries in secret hotel rooms, tucked into pockets beside shiny highways in Kansas City, Kansas that cost their husbands a fortune. Whatever they do, they're phony bitches, with twisted up faces, and Martha Stewart taste in fashion. If they're rebelling, they forgot how. One of them walks by and smiles a pathetic grin. I want to slap the shit out of them and tell their husbands the quickest way to their wives' hearts is with a sharp knife.

Polly comes over beaming like an orgasm and I tell her so.

"You know I'm saving myself for college."

"I was just kidding."

"No, you were right. Xavier and I did it in the barn at his friend's house last night."

"Tell me you're on the pill."

"Of course. My mom put me on it when I turned seventeen. That's how old she was when I was conceived. Which reminds me, I need to throw up now."

"Right. Help me get the glasses from the kitchen." The hallway in Harold's Steak & Brew is dim from the sconces that look like candles and seem to give off less light even though they're electric. They hang on wood panel walls that were in style thirty or forty years ago but sag now like you can see the mold and rot just waiting to creep out through the cracks.

Ian is standing over the butcher block decked out in his grimy white t-shirt and Chief's pajama pants tucked into his black high tops. His hair is greasy and the sweat stands on his forehead like he paints it on there every day to make it look like he's killing himself at work. He carves steaks off a giant piece of meat and chomps on a cigarette. He drinks with us a lot and he and Hank have been friends since they were babies. He coughs in our direction. A flurry of ashes snows down onto the chopping block and soaks into the pooling blood; turns to black specks against the deep red gore. The smell of blood and tobacco fills the air just over the orgy of fried foods hanging in the air like a sponge of hardened grease; persistent as the hot tar they rolled onto the old highway last weekend.

"Smells like death in here." Polly waves her hand in front of her nose.

"I thought it smelled like murder in here." Ian drops the knife through the meat and it hits with a shocking thud.

"He's a teddy bear," I turn to Polly, "when you get to know him."

"That's what they said about Theodore Roosevelt," Polly says. I don't get her joke but smile anyway. She makes me feel dumb when she tells jokes. She grabs a couple of racks of glasses and hands them to me and then grabs the other two herself. Down the hallway I squint to see my way through the dim light and a hot towel hits me right in the back of the head. One side of the rack slips out of my hand and a couple of draught glasses crash to the carpet and bounce against the wall.

Nick says, "Sorry, meant to hit Jake."

"You know we're open for business." The towel hits him in the leg and I walk by, "Hit me again with one of those towels and I'm going to stick a bottle of bourbon up your ass."

"Idiot." Polly follows to the bar.

"You can't talk to me that way. Harold's my cousin."

Turning to look at him from the corner of my eye, "Maybe, but he thinks you're worthless too."

We set the racks on the bar and start putting them away. "Any news from Washburn yet?" Polly asks.

"I get to go. The acceptance came in the mail today. I forgot with all the other stuff at home. I'm excited. I talked to the advisor and they said I should commit to meeting with a tutor since I've been out for a few years. Something about developing study habits, relearning them, I guess. I have to ask Harold though to cut back my hours."

"That won't be a bad thing, right?" she says, glasses ting-tinging as they bump in the overhead racks. "I mean you'll have financial aid to make up for it."

"I don't know. The debt when I get out could make us homeless." The laughter coming out of my mouth sounds far away and I feel a little ashamed. I want a cigarette, a shot would help too. I want to see the kids. I'm tired of working so much.

"I think I know where I'm going to school this fall," Polly said.

"You got another acceptance letter?" The smile on my face is real; I get so happy for her.

"To my first choice school."

She jumps a little when I throw my arms over her shoulders and hug her. Nick whistles from the far side of the bar.

"I'm so happy for you. What was it called again? Middle…march?"

"Middlebury," she smiles, "it's in New England."

"Way to go!"

"Thanks. You still have to go to Washburn though, get out of this job, even though I won't be here to help."

"I just wish that Hank wasn't being this stay at home dad. It doesn't really pay to have someone sit the kids and then he's doing nothing the whole time."

* * *

An hour after the last of the customers leave a group of us talk in the parking lot, smoking cigarettes, Nick has a joint. It floats around and I hit it a couple of times just to wipe the work away from my brain, but Polly, standing beside me, passes it on to the next without a drag.

"So, you're sure you don't want to stop by our house for a little while?"

"Yeah, I'm beat like Jesus."

The laugh that comes out of me sounds like a psychotic ferret through the fog of pot in my head.

"Alright sister, see you later."

"Goodnight, dude," Polly said.

Her car growls out into the night, two red taillights blur into the fog and they become one faint red ball of light sinking into the city.

We all pile into a couple of cars like a brigade of circus clowns on a mission to forget the workweek. Nick's car tears ass up ahead of mine on the old highway. He weaves back and forth to the edges of the road.

At the house a circle of friends jack-jawed madly, stomping feet in laughter, kicking dust across their hard black boots, even the girls were in combat boots. Gina is the only one of them who's actually been in combat. She's been to Afghanistan twice; lost two fingers to shrapnel in the desert during a raid on a prisoner camp by some suicidal Taliban. She could crack any skull here before she was seen coming. Gina straight up grabs Bobby at the nuts with a beer in her other hand and says something I can't hear, but she's laughing and he's trying to. "Hey Gina, gotta handful there?" I said.

"Hey there, baby. How was work?"

"Ready for a drink."

Inside at the kitchen sink, through smoke and a rattle of loud conversations, there are three people I don't recognize. They look out of place, neat Saturday night clothes, hair teased up with gel and pomade, what Polly's calling Product, which is also a local band a friend of ours is in. He's here in the corner brooding over something meaningful. A couple of guys are talking to him but he stares at the table and nods once in a while. He's a big Buddha type presence but quick to violence. Walking over to the fridge through bodies packed like sardines, I see Wes, our psycho Buddha, slap his hands on the table and stand up. His knees bump it and raise one end nearly tipping all the shit on the table which would make the mess of the century, with all the half full glasses of booze, leavings from one of Hank's tweaker projects that involved stripping wires and sorting the colored plastic into piles. He pushes through the crowd and goes outside.

"No fucking way." Looking at the three strangers in the kitchen, Stevie becomes familiar.

"How you be, lady?"

After not seeing him for more than two years I have to hug him to make sure he's real. Over at the table, Hank winks at Stevie while I'm hugging him. Hank's been suggesting swinging or a threesome for like a year, and I know that's what's on his mind when he flips that lid at Stevie. And hell yes, if I had the chance I would do Stevie right there in front of God and everyone. Well, if Polly were here I would take it to the bedroom.

Stevie tells me the two guys he's with are friends of his from Washburn.

"I'm going to Washburn this fall."

"Alright. Way to go." Stevie takes a drag from his friend's cigarette; a little strange in this crowd.

I hear out of the background, "I bet they share the other guy's dick, too." The voice sounds like Rick's and I hope Stevie didn't hear it because he's a brutal mother, when he's pushed. Looks soft as hell though.

Hank's driving to blackout fast. His confidence got crazy when he blacked out. He told me once after a night in the ether, that he felt like Hitler at the Nuremberg rallies when he got to that point, minus the putting people in ovens. He comes jump-dancing over to us to the beat of the metal on the stereo. "Stevie, you bitch, where you been?"

"Working man. What's up with you?"

"Can I get some of that Tequila?"

The two friends of Stevie look like they want to fit in so bad. They smile and shake their heads to the music and laugh when Hank calls Stevie a bitch, which is often.

"So, when you going to join the Marine's, you motherfucker?" Stevie says.

"Oh shit, I love this song."

Heavy guitar rips across the room.

They all start nodding their heads.

"What is this?" One of Stevie's friends wants to know, to belong.

"My Sister's Machine." Hank says this without looking at the guy.

"This song's fucking shit," Stevie said.

"Fuck you man," Hank says and looks at his friends, "if I never found this guy he'd still be listening to Tori Amos and probably emo now."

"L7, Shitlist. Remember that tune buddy?"

"Yeah, I put it on the P.A. at the grocery store in Sand Creek when we came back from that Gruntruck show in Kansas City." Hank looks at the two guys, "We got chased out of the store with brooms by the old lady that ran the place. 'You freaks go back home.'"

"She was hilarious. Probably tells that story at every holiday with her family." Stevie laughs and high fives Hank. "You ever find my Circus of Power cassette?"

"Give it up man, that shit sucked."

"Hank, get over here." Rick's looking for Hank to do some shots out of a bottle of vodka. Hank jumps through the rooms on an invisible pogo stick.

"Come on, we came here to get fucked up," one of Stevie's friends says to the other. He's shoving the bottle of Tequila they brought into the other dude's chest.

"You going to introduce me?" I say to Stevie. His arms look huge and tight.

"Sorry, this tall freak over here is Grime and the one in the pink polo shirt is Kerry."

Grime tears the bottle of tequila away from Kerry and pulls a big shot. He slams the bottle on the counter and turns to the sink. "Easy there, fella." I say and hope he doesn't put the puke-meat of his belly into my sink. He makes a move like he's going to. His throat recoils. His torso spasms and he burps out a toxic cloud of tequila and whatever he'd eaten for supper.

"So, my girlfriend works in the student loan department at Washburn. If you want any help with stuff like that we could get together, you, me and her and get it all sorted out for you. Be a big help, I think," Stevie says. He turns to Grime, "You going to be alright?"

Grime just nods his head.

"Write me down your number, so I can get hold of ya. We have to use the phone at Harold's, so I'd have to call you."

"No phone?"

"Can't afford it."

"Sure, here's my number," he scribbles on a paper from his pocket, Hank jumps over to us again, Stevie says, "if my girlfriend answers her name's Beth, so don't think you've got the wrong number."

"She's some hot little fox with a friendly little box, I bet." Hank said and grabbed the bottle of tequila from behind Grime and looked at Stevie, with his free hand made a V and flapped his tongue through it.

"Jesus, Hank," I apologize with a look, "Thanks, maybe with the student loans we could get a phone line in here."

"Even a prepaid cell would be good. You'll need it."

The night spirals out around me. I get to bed somehow and wake up forgetting how the night ended. I'm still in my clothes and cold on the bed. I put my hands in my jeans pockets. The paper crinkles in my hand. I pull it out to see what it is. Stevie's phone number. Hank snores behind me. I put Stevie's phone number back in my pocket and am happy. I'm going to college and getting out of this trailer.

END

IDLER AT THE WINDOW

Now, that there, is a chill in the air. The smell of fires in the homes in the neighborhoods of the city. The dirty slush ice piled high in the curbs of the avenues which run quiet with the sounds of whimpering vehicles pushed hard through the previous days' heavy snows. They stare blank eyed from the windows of high apartments listening to crooning Bowie drinking remnant volumes of gin or vodka, nectar and Schnapps'. They try on forgotten clothes pilfered one stinking garment at a time from the downtown thrift shop. They are poor but only in spirit. He is employable beyond his ambition but feigns reluctance and hides days in this apartment where he shuffles to and fro stopping always at the large window in the living room to look down on the giant ant people a few floors down. He wrote a poem over the man shoveling his drive in the hard biting wind yesterday morning. The man thoroughly enjoying his time "playing" in the snow so that he could get to work on time, so that his kids would have a place to live, to eat, to sleep; warm. The man broke his shovel trying to stab through the ice that gave up only small shards, fought the molded black plastic scoop of his meager shovel. But the man in the apartment identified with it and discarded it, all of it, the dutiful father, the inadequate shovel, and the immovable ice.

"Yes, Bethany, it is true. I have survived four days now on rations of peanut butter, crackers, ramen soup, and an assortment of booze. We fear, Yvette and I, that she may become pregnant for all of the heathen lust we have indulged in to date."

"I don't want to hear you talk about my sister that way."

"What can I say. The cabin has a fever and it is contagious."

"Just put Yvette on the line."

"Wish I could but she's playing in the tub presently."

"So?"

"We made a new rule, "No electronics in the bathroom." There was an incident with the power drill, a wooden globe and toilet water."

Silence.

"I nearly tazed by balls off with a power tool."

The phone went dead.

He looked at the flashing phone with her name and the duration of the call and pulled the empty line up to his ear, "I love you."

Wet feet smacked the wood floor all down the long narrow hall lit in the flickering candlelight and sucking in the sounds of the sullen Bowie album. Yvette peered around the corner with her towel tied around her chest. "Who was that?"

"Who was what?"

"On the phone?" The towel came loose and she struggled to pin it with her biceps as she pulled her wet, black hair into a ponytail.

"Let it fall."

And she did.

END

KNUCKLES' BROKEN PROMISE

I told you once but it looks like you're going to make me tell you again. Don't give a fuck about the weather, the birds, the trees; whatever. The point is small and if you pay attention you might not miss it this time. I was minding my own business walking out of the post office. What? Did they ask me if I wanted the package insured? Shut up and listen. Did they ask me if I wanted the package insured? From what floor window did your mama drop you out of? I was minding my own business not messing round with no mess around and see this guy beating the shit out of my car. Said, "Hey, buddy. What the fuck you think you're doing?" Accept it wasn't a question, a capiche? I knew what this guy thought he was doing and I was there to set him straight.

He yells, "Hey fuck off brother, this ain't your concern."
"Brother? I ain't your fucking brother." I said, pulled the gun from my waistband, "Matter of fact I ain't no one's brother." What? How'd I get the gun if I just came out of the post office? Don't they have metal detectors? What are you fucking stupid? You the plot police all of a sudden? All of a sudden the gun in my waistband gotta jive with me telling you just moments ago that I was coming out of the post office? You probably still want to know if I got the package insured. I spit on the ground in your general direction, man. Not as a slight on you but just on your thought processes. You sure your momma didn't tape a fork to your hand when you was wee and set you off in the line of an electrical socket? Just checking, bud. Anyways, I pulled the gun from my waistband and calmly told the prick to cease and desist. What'd he do? He comes walking at me with the tire iron he's been using to fix my windows. Well, well, well at that point what I had was a classic case of self-defense not to mention destruction of personal property. I squeezed a couple of rounds into the man and watched him die right there in the street. Did he make a noise? You with the fucking questions, what are you Alex Goddamn Trebek? Is this fucking Jeopardy or candid camera or something? I tell you he sound like a yellow toed warbler, I get some green, a fistful of the ol' benjamins as the niggers would say. Eh, fuck you and your racism. You can point a finger at me when you stop locking your doors at the drive through when you see a black man walk by. I know you do it, you fucking sandal wearing, bar and grill patronizing suburb rat. To answer your question, no he didn't make a fucking noise and if he did…there were too many innocent bystanders screaming apocalypse to hear anything but the sound of my own thoughts. Adding up the cost of those windows that little prick had bashed in for me. Wondering how cheap it is to actually stop another man's heart. Cost of bullets, cost of gun. Quite a value I'd say. Oh, don't get all melodramatic on me, I didn't shoot the

pope. It wasn't your mother. You know we're only a few decades out of a time when the majority of your unscrubbed, rough, frontier types lived by a certain moral code whose justices could always be meted out with a pound of lead and no mass media machine droning on from fat ass sloth bacon lipped assholes who are gonna tell you the right way to live. Get me a gun. Get me a big ole gun to blast the tv's out of the planet. Turn off the PR shit and get back to letting people live and sort out their own goddamn problems. What happened next? This is what happened next. Sorry, I got off on a tangent. Tends to happen when some pencil dick keeps asking these questions. I calmly opened my car door and brushed the glass off my seat, got in and drove down to the bank like I told Dolly I would when I left the house this morning. I wasn't going to stick around and watch the poor bastard rot on the sidewalk. Was I worried about the police? I'm laughing in your general direction because I keeping hearing a whine like a fly buzzing, a fly with shit for brains. I wasn't. The police would find me. They know where I live. What? No. They know where everybody lives. Eventually. Right? If they needed to talk to you they could find you probably in less than an hour, right. Unless we was talking 'bout some cop related to that fly, with the shit for brains keeps interrupting my story. Like I was saying, they'd find me if they needed some answers. Until then I was going to finish the day I had planned before that little incident. Ah, alright, alright. Shit, you're like a child. No, I didn't get the package insured. I thought, fuck it. Something happens, wasn't meant to be. Right? Now, should I carry on or do you wanna talk about the size and colour of the shit I took this morning while I was reading your obituary? No? Okay. When I got to the bank you'll never believe who I run into. Do I still have the gun? My god, you're a dim bulb, what are you about 15 watt? Three way? What's your brightest setting? Can we put it on that? Of course I still had my gun. It's my gun. What am I, going to toss it out the window like some severed cock just 'cause I spilled a little blood? It's my gun. So, yeah. I still had MY gun. You're looking at me like you can't believe I was going to carry it into the bank. Let me stop you right there, rube. Yes, I took my gun into the bank. No, I don't give a fuck. But like I's saying, I run smack into Yessiree Bob and he's got a truckload of civilians reaching for the ceiling while he empties out the teller drawers. Well, I never did like him so much and as he was in the midst of a class A felony I thought I'd do the neighborly thing and put a couple rounds in the old con. Can't imagine the look of surprise that shook him while he had his head poked out of his mask smiling in recognition of an old war comrade and him calling out, "Hey, Knuckles…" and then realizing as he's waving hello that I was sending him a 9mm telegram as the crow flies. I must a bounced one off his shotgun barrel cause the bank teller he was harassing flinched and hit the counter head first. She got back up but was clutching her upper arm like it was a turkey leg she was about to rip off and tear into. Well, I went up to the cashier window and asked, "Pardon me, but would you mind getting four-hundred dollars out from my account and I'll be on my way?" She looked at me as though I'd asked her to fellate a mustang and still clutching her bicep which I kind of felt bad about but mostly not because the real idol of her torment lay dead at her feet. If anything she owed me one, take the money right out of your own account there little sister and we'll call it square. I snapped my fingers in front of her blank stare and could not muster the little beads of attention so I said excuse me and went out to the streets again. I guess I'd go grab a cheap burger and head home. Wait for the cops. All in a day's work, right? All I was going to do was run a few errands and go back home in time to crack a cold one in front of the set. Big game. Put a lot of green down on our home team. But a bunch of low-life cunts got in my way; as cunts are wont to do. So I bet I'd get home just about the time some greasy dick from the precinct was hauling his ass up the stairs to my front door. But you know what? He never showed. I sat down, switched on the game and didn't hear a knock at the door all night. I even opened the fucker and poked my nose into the hall just to edify for my own self that I hadn't made the short list of possible suspects in the daylight shooting of an insane vandal. I checked that hallway each time I got up to piss. Our home team, as you know, stomped the shit out of those sack maggots from the bay. They play hard, our boys in yellow. I put my head on my pillow that night, the first time in a-half-a-dozen years not worrying about nothing. I was gonna sleep like a baby. Until the knock on my door. "You ain't no greasy dick," I said with my eye shoved into the peephole. The gun, where'd I set it? I'd never seen the guy on the other side of the door before but he was certainly at the address he was looking for. The odds of my staying out on parole were quickly dwindling today. Invite him in. Make it look like an aggravated robbery. Make it look good.

END

MALCOLM'S APPLE TREE

Squat beside the foundation in the balmy strain of first light chirping crickets beneath the Coswel bedroom window rubbed their ratcheted wings. They played the same soothing adagio they had struck up at the witching hour. As the timer on the dryer in the basement kicked on there was a pointed pause amongst the trilling ensemble. Nestled in their grassy idyll a few paces from the dryer exhaust that hung like a roman nose off the concrete foundation they kicked up the tempo responding to the rise in ambient temperature. Maggie Coswel rose from bed neatly tucking the cotton sheet and linen blanket under her pillow; the first of many furtive activities she would undertake so as not to wake her sleeping husband. She used both hands to shift the lock on the window and slowly dialed the tiller. The window quietly swayed a few inches into the dawn. One more clandestine errand accomplished.

The chirping seemed to be in stereo now. To her delight, Hubert did not stir. Maggie turned into the master bath and using two hands shut the door wending through chafing screeches and scritches. "Damn you, bastard hinges," she said. Still his chest rose and fell under the linen blanket now, sharply outlined his modest belly in the silhouettes that moonlight passing off of mirrors hanging from three walls relayed.

* * *

He dreamed:
Hubert dandles his grandson Albert on his knee. The November morning lays a frost over the skylights softening the glare of the sun in the clear blue sky. Hubert sings an old country and western song while baby Albert bounces and laughs.

Back east in Kansas City, Albert studied photographs in the sweeping album that was the unqualified narrative of the family saga as regarded his childhood. It was a four volume set of photos and documents culled from the corners of suffocating attics and mothball bureaus stationed across the country. Many years ago the tireless work of his grandma's creaky fingers on her IBM Selectric provided captions under each photo with crucial time and place information unprejudiced by the renown or obscurity of the twinkle in time.

Photos of himself in soft focus were fixed in the walloping book between a cardboard sheet and plastic film that made a zipping racket when peeled apart. Faces were cut off by the end of the lens, eyes glowed red for unknown reasons. It was an out of body memory. He looked back on his life through photographs taken by someone older who stood taller.

This ritual before going to see his Grandpa Hubert and Grandma Maggie reminded him of their connection. Without it he was young and in no need of the wisdom of the aged. He had a long drive ahead of him, enough to listen to two hours of Finnegans Wake.

The first bump in the road came in a single lane of construction work a half hour into the trip. A steady seventy-five m.p.h. had been retarded to thirty. The exhaust from the Mercedes M hypnotized him as it roiled and dissipated. The audiobook began to skip, the traffic sputtered to sporadic standstills. "Only a fadograph of a yestern scene. Only a fadograph of a yestern scene. Only a fad…" The disc couldn't un-stick itself. He ejected it and flipped it over to examine the brains of the thing. It had tree rings all the way across. The thought that he might have an unhealthy preoccupation with Joyce's magnum opus lay in a notebook buried in a box in his basement. He would have to stop in Lawrence to pick up a new copy. Blowing another ninety dollars on "The Wake" would sting his wallet but a plan was a plan and that day he planned to listen to "The Wake." He was going to be late.

* * *

Hubert's eyes opened to the creamy colors of their bedroom. Sunlight cascaded onto the coast of the continent a thousand miles away, climbed like the devil over the mountains of Appalachia and fell breathless upon the Midwest jogging into the city limit. The light stared into the bedroom window. There was no alarm because it was simply time to get up. The smile on his face was the remnant of his dream. "Maggie, where are you?"

She heard his voice in the basement but couldn't make out words for the thumping dryer beside her. If it's important he'll come find me, she thought. Then her imagination kicked in. As she finished the last curl in her hair the purple bruise on the back of her hand spooked her, turned her into the mare that bucked when the first thunderclap bolted from dark clouds on the edge of town; pressed her to see if Hubert was okay.

The steam floating into the hall was friendly fire harnessed in the water heater and distributed at will. She went to the kitchen to read the paper. "Good morning Hubert," she said walking away.

Hubert smelled coffee slipping in under the scent of shampoo they'd pilfered from a hotel in Kansas City last weekend.

They had been overnighting for a family reunion that was to double as a welcome home shindig for Albert. Lieutenant Vlimt was delayed at a base in Kentucky though and missed the welcome entirely. He was expected at his grandparents' house any time this morning.

In pressed black slacks, snakeskin belt, and button-down pink grapefruit shirt Hubert entered the kitchen. At eighty-eight years old he still kept his chin up balancing the feather of pride on his nose he'd put there after steaming across the Pacific to beat back the Japanese Imperial Navy.

The table sparkled like a firework with sunlight ricocheting off the silver, china, glass salt & pepper shakers, and the glass each of milk, orange juice, and water for the two of them. Maggie sat in front of a plate full with biscuits and gravy, eggs, and on a smaller plate toast without butter. She put a piece of toast in front of her lips just to smell it. Some people preferred flowers. These were the days they spent their lives hustling for since back when a nickel a day was a manageable wage.

He had a plate of flapjacks and link sausages in his hand. The coffee was waiting to wash down dessert that this morning was a bran muffin with a dollop of butter. "What time do you think he'll be here? What time is Malcolm gonna be here do you think?" Hubert said.

She put a lilt in her voice when he stumbled over details. "Not Malcolm, his son, Albert."

This time with vigor he said, "Lieutenant Vlimt, our hero come home again."

* * *

He slipped away again:

Albert was peculiar in the audio book section. He'd take a step or two to the left or right looking for the book on disc. Mozart played from the ceiling but had no currency; it was advertising, just part of the brand of the national bookseller. "We move units, not ideas. How's that for a slogan? Then again, people don't buy paperbacks of classics to impress their neighbors." He said it to a petit teenage girl obviously struggling to grasp the subtlety of make-up. She looked like a jester to him or a whore at Mardi Gras. Afraid of falling to the floor, purple eye shadow clung for its life to the skin around her eyes. But points for matching it to the scarf around her neck keeping her warm in this unseasonable heat.

"Help you find anything?" The clerk said.

"Nick, just looking." He did this to see how competent retailers were.

Nick looked at his badge like he had just met himself. Then he blushed.

He would note the encounter later on his lunch in the windowless break room. He'd scribble the details hastily while tippling coffee and gnawing at biscotti sticks.

He would read Your Way To Success: Believe Yourself by General R. Sunday Firckwurst.

Nick began to sidle off, "If you do need assistance, just ask." Albert made no motion to suggest he heard the last thing Nick had said. He did notice, however, that Friendly Mr. Nick was watching him from the end of the aisle

* * *

He was present once again. Hubert scanned the front page of the paper bouncing between headlines of tax breaks, sewer repairs, and a journalist kidnapped in Toronto. It was a windy high plains morning and the screens battered against the window frames every once in a while as they made their way through breakfast. She, guiding him like his own personal Beatrice.

"Do you remember the summer we bought this home?" She said. She had a half of one biscuit in the palm of her hand and was applying a precise dollop of fresh raspberry jam that Hubert's sister-in-law had jarred herself last month. Into her 79th year she still savored the taste and texture of cold jam on a steamy biscuit. It made her morning. "That summer when the Werpol Building was demolished downtown? And we moved into this house but took lunch downtown to stand in the crowd of onlookers?"

He looked out the window beside her. The world outside the window was just an image; just a painting he was looking at that had no meaning, no metaphor, and no reference. He blinked at intervals so distant that Michelangelo could have painted saints upon his corneas. He looked out the window into the image and didn't understand why the painting moved.

"When we moved in and then Albert was born?" She said.

He smiled.

"And Malcolm planted the apple tree? So we could watch it grow as Albert would?" She said.

He said, "That was when the Packard finally broke down for good." She stared at her sweet husband's sugar coated hair thickset as the moment she saw him in their cardinal affair. A dump truck with Pity in the driver's seat deposited a heap in her throat. He finished, "And Edward and Lucy Govinki perished in that train wreck west of town."

The sand load in her throat fell down her hour glass and her throat cleared just to say, "That was a different summer."

He returned to the occasion of their conversation, "What time do you expect Albert?"

Maggie was up from the table now and walking out of the kitchen, "We've got to pick up the dry cleaning tomorrow too." She didn't say, "So don't let me forget."

* * *

Hubert wandered inside his head again:
Albert walked back to his car and passed a trucker filling up. "Hey pal, thanks for smoking," he said. The man in the Realtree hat and matching jacket flipped him off and pulled himself up into the cab of his semi-truck.

Back on the interstate and out of the mire of construction zones disc nine of Finnegans Wake diverged recklessly around the car while Albert shot a text to his Dad to let him know that he was sitting in Hubert and Maggie's driveway. In fact, he was not. His father so detested tardiness that he would take them to church a second time if they were even a verse late for the opening song. So Albert lied, which he found easy to do in a text.

The rig ahead of him was losing pace with traffic, maintaining the lane but bouncing between the lines like a pinball. Albert kept an eye on it and an eye on his text. He reread it many times without sending it, his thumb hovered over the green button. He worried his dad might call his grandparents' house, find out his text was a lie. He thought about the notion of the landline telephone; how his grandparents talked about party lines at the birth of the technology, how it was on its way out as a communications tool, he visualized a million conversations floating through the sky.

"Forshapen his pigmaid hoagshead, shroonk his plods foot…Me seemeth a dragon man." "The Wake" diverged recklessly. The rig, the same.

* * *

Hubert was jarred from his absence by the recollection of the phone call Malcolm made to them that morning, all those years ago. "Are you sitting down, Dad?" Malcolm said in the phone.

"What is it, son?" Hubert said.

"Albert was killed," Malcolm said.

Hubert was sitting in the same chair, then, as now.

Maggie watched a lark dance among the old trees whose morning shadows laid against the blond grass.

"Do you remember when Malcolm cut down the apple tree?" she said.

A tear fell from Hubert's eye and brought with it many friends.

END

MORNING

Who brought all those flowers while I was sleeping? She wondered. There must be a dozen unopened cards stuffed in those arrangements, she noted. I wish I knew who brought them. I dreamt so many people came through here last night, she thought. Then it occurred that maybe she hadn't dreamt them visiting.

A skid mark from the sole of the nurse's left shoe fanned out across the waxed cream floor. From the pillow she stared at it and hoped it wouldn't be the last thing she ever saw. She felt so tied to the bed that she thought they had become one in the middle of the night. The backs of her arms, where triceps used to stretch, seemed to be in a constant state of free fall; falling through the bed, falling through the floor, falling through the ground, falling through the earth. The skid mark breathed like a lung. She couldn't. Not as easy. As if there were a cataract, it all began to blur. Her eyelids were pinned open ignoring her heart's desire to blink, to wet the eyes and clear the way. The smudge began to spread.

Without moving her body she thrust her eyes to the ceiling and became the little girl that laid in bed tense in a tantrum. She felt heat rise from her body, a simmering mirage in the slanting sunlight. The word of the day was NO. It raced through her mind. He was sleeping in the chair beside her. For the first time in years she had woken up before him. Why now? She was mad, such that she felt her entire body quiver and vibrate but didn't make so much as a whisper of a sheet rustle. And all the while, NO NO NO. I don't want to do this, not now. WAIT!

* * *

See, Reader, love is like this. Hard. Hard, hard, hard. You think you've got it all locked up. The world, while it may not exactly be your oyster, the world puts you in a place where you get to love and be loved by somebody. If you're lucky, you get to add more people to that little world. And then something happens; someone moves far away, someone takes a new job, or someone…someone gets sick, real sick. Someone has to start taking medicine that kills them while it makes them better, the ratio isn't set in stone, every body's different. Sometimes the medicine kills someone more than it makes them better. And you gotta be there through it all. Or you don't. You could chicken out, move on to greener pastures and live a less stressful existence while the one you said you loved falls apart. And then you could look your chickenshit self in the mirror every day and lie to yourself that you deserve happiness.

When what you've really done is taken that cancer outta the poor little animal you said you loved and put it right inside your heart. No, Reader, love is hard.

* * *

    She could see him if she turned her eyes to her left, could watch him sleep; his chest rise and fall under his black fleece coat that he'd laid over himself for a blanket. His shoes were still on. She was glad the television wasn't on. She hated when it was on in the morning even if the volume was muted, hated the way it staled the morning. It felt like the day was just a leftover of yesterday when that happened and not the fresh start that each day deserved. She rolled her eyes toward him, wanting to stay on him if this was the moment. But she started to cry. He breathed slowly, rhythmically. The little girl throwing tantrums a moment ago now sobbed, desperate. She looked away to the right side of her bed trying to look out the window but only able to hold her eyes up for a moment before weakness brought them back to the dark lung smeared across the waxed cream floor. NO NO NO. Her heart broke. Without metaphor or romance, the wind had been knocked out of her. She said I love you, I love you, I love you, I love you like a wind rushing through her mind, through the reels and stills of those she held dearest, hoping the messages would be received before they were lost. Images scattered in whirlwinds. The wind flew fast. Her lips opened to speak but all that came out.
    Was the wind.

END

STELLAN BAMBREY

Remember?
When you thought that little tinge was serious?
That you were away in thought, blankly staring through the television as some old black and white program from your grandparents' heyday mumbled low into the living room. You there on the couch slumped down and numb against the tingling cramps building up in your limbs. And you felt that quick shot right up all your bones. Jolted from your gravy mind washed in blue light flickering against the curtains, the back of your head glued itself to the couch cushion. Paralyzed in fear and the virgin cognizance of your own death. The first time the grave lashes on and pulls you in for a dry run. Your heart starts beating again with a rapid thump and your breath digs in like a shell shocked marine

home for the holidays, is it war and peace this life and death? Wake up, Mr. Bambrey. Mr. Bambrey, wake up.

* * *

"Stellan Bambrey?" a man's voice said.

"Yes, mmm hmm," Stellan said.

"This is Victor Martin calling from Porcelain Jowel Insurance."

Stellan shook the sleep out of his eyes. He stared at the rerun of Mr. Ed on the tube and reached for the remote blindly among the clutter on the glass coffee table. He swiped at it and knocked down an empty glass, tipped a half empty bottle of Red with the back of his hand and caught it quickly, making him think of the Golden Glove trophies he saw in Cooperstown when he was a kid. "Did you say Porcelain Jowel?"

"No sir," the man's voice fluttered like a sob, "Portland, Tao, Will Insurance."

That phone call, that late hour. Stellan shrugged it off. Can't talk now, he said. Too many things going on. Will be in touch when the first opportunity arises. He hung the phone up and stared at the ceiling. Thunder.

He dug his cell from his jean pocket searching for the number. Had they erased her voicemail announcement message yet? He wondered. He wondered what kind of damage he would do to his own psyche if he listened to it even as he dialed the number and waited with heavy breath for the sound of her voice. Once more. As it rang he clumsily stumbled through the room pulling cables and wires trying for the voice recording machine he used to record songs that popped into his head. He found it. Popped it open to check the tape. Popped it shut and clicked down the record/play buttons. "Hello," she said.

He froze.

"Hello?"

What? He couldn't speak, like when you cry so hard that no sound can be made to translate the pain causing it.

"If you're looking for Heather, I'm sorry."

"How do you…"

She sighed, "I should tell Audorcell to give me a new number."

"Audorcell…" he fumbled the thoughts, "gave you her number."

"It's just a phone number sir." She paused, "I'm sorry if you're looking for her but you must know she's died.

It's not just a phone number, he thought. "She is my wife."

Silence. "I'm sorry," she said. "I'm going to let you go. I'm going to call Audorcell in the morning and get a new number. You're the tenth person I've had to…" she hung up the phone.

He looked at it flashing the phone number and two minutes five seconds. That's all it took. She wasn't going to answer his calls again. The finality stunned him and he felt cheapened as a plastic grocery sack twisted in a fence because life's biggest moment hit him on a cheap plastic phone.

Stellan went off to the bedroom, but to motivate himself to sleep, he found was impossible. Eventually he curled up in a blanket on the floor on her side of the bed. When he woke there in the morning, stubble beard, and chalky whisky mouth he sadly felt the erection pushing against the floor.

He tossed and turned morosely jerking off thinking about the last time they had sex, made love, fucked in their bed, on the floor, in the shower, in the car in the garage after a new year's party. He came in the blanket and stretched and yawned. His eyes watery and aching to focus through the dim bedroom.

Her picture pierced the half guilt of his post orgasm walk to the shower.

The water thudded against his chest and he leaned into it until it beat against his closed eyelids. Blood-black visions strobing in his eyes threw him into vertigo and he wobbled in the shower. He stood there until the water ran cold, until the gooseflesh covered him head to toe. What do I do today? What on earth is there to bother about? It's about satisfaction. It's about dulling all pain. He made his way to the Tacqueria in the slums. They had big food and hot, fresh sauce. And even though it was only ten in the morning and his stomach would likely revolt in revenge, he would eat his favorite food and it would break the loop of desperation in his heart.

END

TALK OF SEX OVER WINE:
WRONG PLACE, WRONG TIME

It was in a New York City restaurant called the Queen Juliana that she first heard his name. Her parents had just returned from a business trip that led them all around Europe and into Moscow. They were jet lagged and distracted by a lingering argument that Emelia could tell was simmering only for her sake. Her mother took her hand from across the little round table and patted it dearly. Em took this as some codified signal she thought she was supposed to know. One that her mother must certainly have explained to her at some point in the distant past. Distance being a relative thing because of Em's age. Being only 24 it is hard for a person of any stripe and upbringing to intimate a long traveled road. Though, with a little empathy and guiding hand it would not be impossible to think of a life lived where the moments from one to the next string along in the time bending sagas of despair. That some events are so monumental they seem to draw out the swing of the second hand so that a legal second to the person assaulted with these betrayals feels like they are travelling in a bubble where they do not actually move through time but stand outside of it for many years until the moment breaks, the bubble bursts and the person is returned a second later but many years worse for the wear. In her heart she apologized to her mother for not knowing the signal. Should she alert the authorities of her mother's imminent danger and from whom or what is her mother endangered by? She flinched and her hand shrunk from her mother's.

"We met a man in Brussels we think you would get on with quite well," her father said, biting salad from his fork. He licked at the dressing on his lip like a perverted frog coming on his lily pad with each swallowed fly.

"Harvey. We said we wouldn't bring him up," Em's mother Gaye said.

"Bring him up. Ehh, what's the harm. Look at her, she's miserable, working in that ambulance chaser's sty out in the burbs. She needs a man. Not these guitar playing poseurs with boyish dreams of sports cars and record deals."

"Harvey." Gaye scolded.

"What? She needs a real man, not a breast feeding, locker room wanking, criminally insane manchild looking for topless female nudity in the glossy pages of the National Geographic."

"Inappropriate. Harvey," Gaye stood up and threw down her napkin for effect. Em slid out from the table and into the bubble, she stayed right where she was but still she felt herself removing from the table. Her mother continued to yell all the way to the front of The Queen Juliana.

"Excellent. Sorry honey. I'm just concerned. When's the last time you had a good lay?"

"You don't see how that's not right?" Em said.

Harvey laid his fork on his plate and waited. What now, what now in this melodrama of a life. At what age, he thought, would it be okay to discuss this stranger's needs and wants? "I don't know anything about you. I don't know what to say to you."

"How about not starting with, 'you look like shit. I found some dick for you.'"

"Sugar, please. Calm down."

"Really, okay. Welcome back to New York daddy. Would you like to know about my sex life? I ate out my girlfriend in the locker room at Michel's Wellness Center last night cause it was near closing time and I didn't think anyone would notice."

"Okay. Alright. That's enough. I'm your father and I'm asking you not to embarrass yourself."

"Embarrass myself. You fucking pig." Em stood up and started toward the door. "Why don't you remember that before you fucking tell me I need to get fucked. Fuck you." And she was gone.

The waiter came with the check, "Sir, the chef is unable to prepare the dinner you've requested tonight. With regrets we ask that you resume your reservation at a later date." The waiter glanced reflexively toward the door where Em was throwing herself into her coat. She knocked over a cane holder by the front door with her purse. Then clumsily burst through the door into the warm spring night.

Harvey motioned for the waiter to bend to hear him, "Listen you smug fuck, I could buy you and the rest of your immigrant family. You couldn't get your foot in the door with my daughter," and at this prepared his voice for projection as if he were speaking to the last row of Yankee Stadium without a mic, "SO GET THE FUCK OUT OF MY FACE!"

Em sat on the couch in her house on the end of Paris Street in the nightclub riddled neighborhood of Spar Beach. There was no beach to speak of and the only sand around was in the ash trays outside of the shops and deli's or in the winter when the plows came through.

Alita was a research assistant Em met at the toy store uptown looking for a Garvey The Policeman doll for her nephew. Alita was singing quietly down the aisle and twisting her sunglasses in her fingertips and wearing shorts and a one piece swimsuit being then employed as a blouse.

Alita sat on the couch beside Em. "You smell like wine and adultery." Alita said.

"I have not."

"Incorrect."

"Okay but it was only once and it didn't really count cause I don't like boys."

"Then why did you marry one?"

"I don't know. All the girls were doing it. It seemed like a funny thing to do. I didn't think he thought I was serious."

"It was a Catholic wedding. It didn't dawn on you to think the joke was being missed when the priest did his magic spells?"

"This really got going. Is this how a proper domestic dispute begins?"

"I don't know. Let's call up the hotline." Alita grabs her phone and mimes dialing, waiting on a dial tone and twisting her hair and blowing bubble gum bubbles. "Um, hello Straight Eye for the Queer Gals and Guys? How do the straights do it up when they want to have a fight? Oh, I need to tell the bitch she don't do me no good no more? Thanks Straight Eye. You're the best." She operatically punches the end call button with her index finger, "Bitch you done don't do me no good no more."

"Must have got the black operator this time, last time it was all, 'Sincerely Margaret I believe we have reached a most formidable impasse, take Shelley and Byron up to your mother's in the Hamptons and we can begin the daunting process of invoking the prenuptial agreement. If you remember the exit is there beneath the ram's head I shot in Kartoum on our safari."

Alita laid her head into Em's lap and closed her eyes. They talked a few hours about things new couples talk about.

END

THE HIGH PRICE

"If you think I won't do it…" BANG. Alan had no intention of finishing his sentence. Teddy had no chance to plead for his life and the issue was resolved.

"I knew it wasn't going to be pretty," Frank said. They'd picked up Teddy that night to square the death of their friend, guitar player Roger Haupps. "Where'd you get that thing?" Frank said.

"It was lying out at Roger's house. I picked it up after everyone had left when we went to check on his house." Alan said.

* * *

They had picked up Teddy at the Elmhurst downtown and drove him out to his country house. Before they got to his front door Alan pulled the gun on him, "You killed my friend," he threw a bag of white dope at Teddy's feet, "that was your weapon. No court will convict you, this is justice—capital J. If you think I won't do it…" BANG. "You're wrong. Junky," Alan spat on his forehead and took the money from Teddy's inside jacket pocket. Worried about detective work, Frank wiped Teddy's forehead with his silk handkerchief. Alan tossed the gun into the hedge and he and Frank made their way to Heathrow. Their flight was scheduled to depart in an hour for Berlin; another show on a tour that was beginning to take its toll.

END

THEY OUGHTTA MAKE A LAW

It was so rainy that night I had a hard time following you home. I waited in the parking lot for twenty minutes while you sat in a booth with that girl you work with. You were waiting for the rain to die down I guess, but if you'd had a chance to check the weather you'd have seen that a storm was pouring down all the way across the state.

Finally, you made a run for your car and I saw the puddles explode around your shoes. Your umbrella nearly flew out of your hands when you sat down in your car and I felt sorry that I laughed a little. It was probably 9:30 by the time we left McDonald's where you put in another long day.

When you did start driving it was hard to see even with the wipers on full speed. I hunched over my steering wheel as I imagine you were doing also just to try to stay in the correct lane. The streetlights colored the entire street. After eight city blocks traveling between fifteen and twenty miles an hour you finally pulled into your apartment complex parking lot. I drove on to the gas station. I ran out of cigarettes waiting for you to leave work and I was a little…off kilter, I guess.

At the gas station the rain seemed to come down ever faster. I didn't want to get wet in my new track shoes. I was breaking them in. I haven't run in eighteen years, not since high school but I thought I'd take it back up. I remember you saying that the shoes looked really cool on the boy you were talking to when I came in to see you last week. You looked really excited to see him and his friends, said that work was really slow and it was nice of them to swing in and talk for a while even though your manager, Christie?, was on your back.

At the gas station, Veronica, the clerk who's always working when I go in at night wanted to talk longer than usual. I told her I had to go, but she had some long story about her cat, Alexandra, being deathly ill, that she probably wouldn't make it and that she didn't know what she would do if she lost her. I told her not to worry, that sometimes the things we love have to die for the fulfillment of the love between the two things. She said that was weird and her saying that made me uneasy to the point of being sick. I told her I really had to get going.

My stomach was hurting from the encounter and I ran to my car in the rain but had to go behind the station to throw up. It was awful, cause the rain was just pooling in the parking lot and my vomit just floated on top of it, not really going anywhere or thinning out. Before I came back to your place I took off my shirt which was soaked anyway and used it to clean off my mouth and blow the rest of the vomit out of my nose.

    I drove shirtless and cold with my damp chest and torso exposed. I smoked a cigarette or two and cranked the defrost on hot but the car is junk and it barely got warm at all. I saw a cop in your parking lot when I pulled in and got worried that something had happened. I nearly threw myself out of the car to rush in and see if you were okay. But then I saw the cop talking to the guy that lives six apartments across from yours and remembered his stereo playing was a nuisance to all of you. I remembered I needed to get some ginger snaps before the grocery store closed so I left the parking lot and picked those up real quick. But when I got to the store they wouldn't let me in because I didn't have a shirt on. I said I'd only be a moment if it was okay but the security guard still said no. I said I'm sorry, I got sick and had to clean up the mess with my shirt. He still insisted on not letting me in. I asked if I could buy one of the college football shirts on the pole by the produce aisle just inside the door and he still shook his head no. I said I had money and that money would get me a shirt and let me in. He asked what was so vital that couldn't wait until I cleaned myself up and had on "the proper shopping attire". I told him I just wanted some ginger snaps to ease my stomach. He pointed to the parking lot.

    I sat in my car for a long minute twisting my shirt and punching the roof of the car. I put the shirt on and it almost made me sick again but this is how the security guard wanted to play it. I confidently strode in with my vomit soaked shirt on and purchased my ginger snaps. On the way out he made some comment about me smelling like a dump. I turned around and said, "It didn't have to be this way you know." He looked at me cross and turned around.

Back in the car I cracked open the ginger snaps and ate them one by one while driving back to your place. I panicked when your car wasn't there anymore. Oh no, what have I done now! I parked and waited under the old oak tree at the end of the lot so that I wouldn't make your neighbors uneasy. If they didn't know I was there they wouldn't have to worry.

I munched on my ginger snaps and smoked until I fell asleep waiting for you. I wonder where you could have gone. I'm sorry I missed you. But I'd wait for you, wait for you no matter what. It got so cold that night. I dreamed a hard dream in which you climbed into my car and made love to me, secretly, silently while I slept. I woke up with a warm stain on my pants and scanned the windows and mirrors to see if anyone was looking. I used the only rag I could find. I rubbed the vomit shirt feverishly over the stain and succeeded only in making it more permanent I believe.

And then you pulled into the parking lot.

Your hair was pulled back in a bouncy pony tail and your sweatpants were rolled at the waist. The sweatshirt with your college logo pulled around you in the wind and your breasts bulged out beautifully. I didn't have to imagine you getting inside and stepping out of these clothes, walking around naked while your shower steamed up the bathroom to just the right temperature. No, I didn't have to imagine it because I could see it all from the retaining wall behind the evergreens.

I was a little confused wondering why, when you took your sweatpants off there was no underwear to be removed also.

The last time I saw you that morning was when you rounded the corner out of your bathroom. The light in your bedroom went on and there was no sign of you after that. I waited a good half hour on the retaining wall. I hopped down and walked beside your apartment. I put my hand to the wall thinking you must be just on the other side of it, maybe sleeping in your bed still butted up against the wall below this window. That's where it was the last time I was in there. I let my hand glide along the wall while I walked back to my car.

The wind was stinging and a tear bled from my eye. I nearly knocked over a landscaper who was crouched down around the corner doing some early autumn trimming of the rose bushes on the front of your apartment. Was he looking in your windows? I worried for your safety. I'd keep an eye on him from my car until he moved on. You shouldn't have to worry about guys like him while you sleep. I'll watch out for you. If your father were still around I know he'd be proud of me. Shake my hand, tell me to keep up the good work looking out for his little girl.

The dream happened again. I wake up. I'm the only person around for miles. There is an echo of the world as it was but it's no longer there. Just an empty shell. Life barely holds on in microscopic forms. The teeming civilization vanished. And the motorcycle on its side in the empty parking lot. Like it was a sign. Here's something to help. A clue. But I have never ridden a bike before and am scared to get on it. I pick it up and stand it upright and just stare at it. And then, always just before I know the dream is about to end the screams and the yelling come from the distance behind me. I never see the faces they come from but they get closer and closer until they must be right behind me, as though if I turned around there would be a mob of madmen waiting to devour me. And I woke up from it the same way, sweating, gasping for air.

It's dark again. Night comes fast these winters. I'll come back in the morning. Make sure you get to work okay.

WAIT! Tomorrow is your day off.
We can spend the whole day together.

END

FROM A HAND YOU'VE ONCE SHAKEN

You are supposed to feel fear. The experience is meant to overwhelm your capacity to understand and organize events—action and reaction. A flash of recognition is confused in the compression of an instant. Fight or flight will be reduced to stillness.

The fist connected with his jaw, left of the chin. A body barreled over him and confidently walked off. He heard laughter from the assailant's companion and then went to black. No audio, no visual. "George?" Cory said. Time was brought back to speed and his brain registered the blow though shock delayed the pain. Players returned to their marks and his absence was unnoticed. "Yeah...Yes?" George said.

In the sharp light of the sun Cory's face was easy to make sense of but not the world surrounding him. He took the hand Cory was holding out and pulled himself to his feet. Soon enough he began to recognize the bay in the background and all of the tourists though they were not the same still became familiar as tourists in his city. Cory looked at him trying to see any sign of damage and then took steps forward passing George to exit the pier. They walked up to catch a bus at Beach Street.

Holding his jaw gently George sat across the aisle from Cory. He tried not to let his eyes become fixed on the floor but couldn't divert his attention from the gum stuck to the floor in front of Cory's shoe. "Where ya staying?" he said.

"I took a reservation at the Nob Hill Motel. Do you know it?" Cory said.

"Know of it." he said. The pain from his jaw made it hard for him to look up from the peach gum. Pissed he stood up as the bus approached their stop.

At George's loft on Jones they sat at a cork top table beside a window. The table clashed so absurdly with the rest of the furnishings Cory like so many other visitors had to ask why George would keep such a thing. George tried to update the response every time but after the fifth time his answer formed its own place in his mind and seemed at times to sit on the table for him to pick up and hand to whomever asked. The answer now relayed was there for the person to inspect and turnover analyzing its makeup, admiring its perfection and brevity while slightly aware of minor imperfections that begged for the person to pursue a less imperfect replacement. Cory was no archaeologist and left the initial answer alone satisfied with it. "The table was used by my mother back in Topeka when she would put together her albums that held all the photos and memories of the places she'd traveled to." George said.

As he told him what the table was George was aware that Cory remembered she'd passed away six years ago this April. He also knew that he remembered that George had moved to San Francisco only a month before she died. She would be 56 forever to the people who didn't know her. Anyone knows though that the moments that make people's lives exist forever still that old codger Death seems to get the only acknowledgement when a person hears of another's demise whom they'd never met. Cory asked how his chin was and took a drink of tea.

"Fine. Fine. How's the tea?" George said.

"Excellent thank you. Did you know the little hoodlum in the Ramones shirt that hit you on the chin?" Cory said.

George shook his head lethargically and the absence of emotion and nonverbal response resonated with deception as he looked at Cory. Even though they'd not seen each other in about a year George was sure that Cory was able to discern a lie of omission. Nevertheless it became a dead issue. Cory thumbed lazily through a copy of the Chronicle on the table barely lifting the corners of the first section to read headlines on subsequent pages. He asked Cory if he'd had a chance to catch up on local news despite knowing the staff of the Nob Hill Motel put out a daily copy of the Chronicle for each room and that Cory had been reading the paper every morning since he was eight perpetuating a childish goal—one he'd confided he thought as a child would get his name in the Guinness Book. He suspected Cory's 'no' was a gesture against his denial of knowing who it was that hit him now forty minutes ago—a pawn pushed forward in answer to

George's pawn all part of the forward movement of their newly resumed never-ending mental tournament which began many years ago at college in Lawrence.

"So, about the letter, you asked me about on the pier...I haven't seen it. You sure you got the address right?" George said.

"Checked it twice." he said

"But if I see it—you want me to shred it before I read it?"

"Yeah, it was full of misdirected emotional diatribes based on inaccurate information." Cory said.

George said he would do his best to kill any curiosity that might otherwise drive him to open the letter and devour it line for line allowing him to build up an uncontrollable rage against his friend. The comment was meant to cover the fact that ever since Cory so strangely showed up on the pier he'd been consumed with paranoia. The coincidence of the two running into each other was too large to overlook.

The room was so anonymous considering Sera could afford much more luxuriant accommodation. As George pushed quietly against her resistance she moaned in whimpers he felt were more for him than she. They'd already done the rough, passionate stuff last night—the first night they'd spent together. In two more days she'd be gone headed to Dallas where her husband thought she was now.

As she slept there with her head on his chest he thought of the punk messenger who brought the delivery to his office earlier that day. He told the punk in his new Ramones shirt that he was glad Joey was dead and that he hoped punk would die with him. The punk not wanting to lose one of the only jobs he could keep and still maintain his anti-growing up look as George saw it did nothing. Sera came to, looked up at George and smiled slightly before getting up to go to the bathroom that was not three feet from the bed.

He stood at the only window that looked out to a parking area which opened onto Pacific Avenue unseen from her corner room on the second floor. He heard her singing quietly in the shower. He could not make out the words but recognized the song though he couldn't recall the title. Dizziness from the champagne at dinner was making waves of his thoughts and he drifted back and forth somewhere between guilt and satisfaction. The rain began to die down as she stepped from the bathroom and George closed the window.

She checked out the next morning after George left and she spent Saturday and Sunday at his place on Jones Street. They did couple things; the park, the theater, dinner at cafes al fresco, and a short tour of Napa. She never took off the ring and he never commented on it. When he dropped her at the airport they kissed goodbye both wishing for one last round in the back of the rented Lincoln. He didn't expect to hear from her for another year or more. They'd keep up through the grapevine.

Cory stood behind George pouring another glass of tea for them both in a gesture to let George deal with his sore jaw. As George gazed out of the window upon the roofline of the buildings across the street he recalled what Sera had told him that second night in the motel room. She told him that Cory would be leaving before she returned from Dallas. She told him specifically that he was coming to San Francisco to meet a potential employee who he was to interview. Even more to the point he now knew why Cory was able to find him at such a seemingly random location. Random is not random when you go to the pier every Friday morning to watch the tourists and joke about it on the phone with your friends who then take it up in their own cities so as to further have something in common with close friends.

On their phones on Friday mornings they'd spent a significant amount of time comparing notes. Cory in Chicago on the Navy Pier describing the person George was quietly observing on Pier 39. "White shorts hanging obscenely below enlarged gut barely covered by pink shirt—polo, right chest text reads Montana—wife studying specialized cartoon tourist map, three kids under four feet tall screaming to get to the Ferris wheel, to see the performing seals etc..." Some mornings they were drunk, some hung-over, some depressed seeking company but always alone in their environment with no connection but the cell phone.

George stood to face him now dealing with the shock of Cory's question which he immediately decided to play as an assumption. If he could somehow bend reality enough for both of them he might be able to save himself from another blow to the jaw or worse. Cory stood looking at him, waiting for a response. George could feel an eternity passing between them and smelled the faint acridity of a dead friendship. "So you're here in place of the letter?" George said.

"No, I'm here in the absence of your response—twice now." he said.

"Twice?"

"You should've got the letter a week ago. And now, you stand here stone faced and looking for a way out of this reality." Cory said.

"I promise you I've got no letter from you and I'm not some chicken-shit whore. I really think you've got some bad information. Sera has not been in this city and if she has she's rudely been and gone without so much as a hello phone call." They stood for a minute not speaking before Cory finally excused himself and went to his motel room.

What else could he do George thought, I played it cool enough—just the right amount of denial and a hint of indignation. I almost slipped and said he'd come out sooner than Sera had led me to believe. Oh well, he'll take care of his business, go back to Chicago and calm down, then hopefully call and tell me how he just doesn't know and all that and that he's just going to have to live with not knowing. "Hey Sera, you got a couple of minutes to talk?" She sighed into the phone before telling him she had Cory on the other line and that he was frantic and crying saying he wants a divorce. George sat at the table in the seat his friend had been in and thought about going out for a drink. "Fuck it. What's the point?" He grabbed his jacket and headed down to the street.

    He walked down to the Irish pub on the corner of North Point Street and took a seat at the bar. Halfway through George's third scotch the bartender threw up his hands and backed toward the other end of the bar from him. George felt the muzzle of a pistol on the back of his head and saw in the mirror through a clutter of half-empty bottles of booze the face of a man in control. Cory didn't say anything to him. Then, nothing.

    George's sister was in town to pack up his things and clean up his loft. She got the last of his mail which had been overstuffed in his box for a week. She threw the bundle on the cork top table and set herself to emptying the kitchen cabinets. After an hour of cleaning things up she fixed a lemonade and sat at the table. The windows were open and a breeze was blowing in of the late summer air. The sun still sat high enough to illuminate all the worldly things in the city. She picked up the bundle of letters and began sorting—unconsciously piling bills apart from personal human things. She set the rest of the bundle down with her left hand and stared for a moment at the envelope in the other. A bent envelope from Cory Murphy burned in her eyes while the tears welled up. She couldn't bring herself to open it. She wanted to. She couldn't.

END

THE SNAKE IN THE HOURGLASS

Those were the days of flying sand. The wind was out of control even by flatlander standards. We were dug into that beleaguered house with blood under our fingernails and open sores on our limbs. To walk outside was to be run through with tiny blades as many as stars.

Roger couldn't hack it in the confined shelter and lit out weeks ago.

I woke in the morning to the sound of sand belting the dry boards of the house. It sounded like sleet. I heard him muttering his incoherent sideways obliteration of language and the last thing he laid into his pack was the pistol. I got up slowly so as not to wake the others. I crept over to Roger, his muttering growing more intense, acute and syncopated. "Roger, are you going?"

"Dog's gotta run. Can't hide in here and wait to die."

"The gun?"

"No bullets. Thing's useless as a weapon. It's so I've got something to remember of this lot."

I put my hand on his WWII surplus backpack. Before the dirt filled our nostrils and made us bleed and scab up in the nostrils that pack had made the whole cabin reek of mothballs and old cloth. "You'll die out there."

"I'll die trying."

"This might pass. You can survive in here 'til it does."

"I'm tired." He turned up his bloodshot eyes and black blood crustied nose, "I'm not alright. I feel insane."

"We all do. But we stand a chance in here. Besides, the door is blocked up with a drift of earth and sand god knows how deep. You open it and we all pay."

"Is that a threat Billy?"

"Fact."

He pushed me out of the way, "I'll go out the tunnel, I'll seal it up behind me and you can stay in your nest with the others."

"You don't know that you can get out through there. Theodore's body is still down there. He could be blocking the whole shaft."

"I'll carve him up and get by."

I put my hand on his wrist to stop him moving the fireplace grate; our entrance to the tunnel. "You can't. We agreed not to touch him."

"What's past is prologue. Ain't that what our boy Teddy used to say?" Roger swatted my hand away and it stung the pocked up wounds on my skin. "I'll leave some meat for you'se guys. Maybe you'll live another week in this nuthouse."

I hadn't been out in the sand for days but my skin had not closed up and the little holes where the sand had beaten me began to run slowly with blood; at first. Roger looked down at my hand and arm, grunted, tore a piece of fabric from his sleeve and handed it to me. "You need to eat. Your blood is thinner than my patience."

I took the cloth and felt a tear in my gland that fought its way back inside the eye. "Thank you," I said and tied the fabric over my skin. He made to get into the tunnel on his belly, head first. "Wait, wait."

He paused, head into the opening of the tunnel poised to leave this womb of death and madness. Without turning, "What Billy?"

"Why?"

"I don't know why. Cause a storm grew. Cause it hasn't stopped. Cause it's planet death. Cause it's a suicide of the mind. Cause god needed a break. Cause the world is tired. I don't fucking know."

"Why are you going out?"

"I broke," he said and sighed so deep I could make out his rib cage under the frail hem of his shirt. I dreamt of killing O'Kief."

"It was a dream. We're under stress. Our minds are bound to lash out in unconsciousness."

"No hippy, I was daydreaming. It was fantasy. I wondered what it would feel like. My morals have slipped out. I have no off switch." And he related the story to me.

* * *

Roger inched back from the mouth of the tunnel in the floor of the fireplace in the creaking cabin squeaking with every inch of sand and dirt that flew to the growing drift laid into its sides. He sat on the floor with his head against the brick chimney. Stared dead eyed at the ceiling with eyes so bloody he looked like some feeble saint overcome with the tears of the lamb in the garden. I recalled my youth at Catholic masses and was saddened by the death of all that mystery swung into my mind riding its chariot of incense and wine.

"O'Kief stirs at the telling of his own death," Roger narrated aloud.

"What the fuck are you guys doing? Why's the grate off the tunnel?" O'Kief woke at a bad time.

"Roger's panicked. He's got something to say."

"I went into the tunnel with Theodore like every other time. Get the water, try to find wood." Roger brought his knees up to his chest and held them there like a kid on a playground thrown out in a dodge ball match. "It was when we first started to get hungry. Not used to it. I never knew that the blood in my stomach, the lining I was crapping out, the ulcers that twisted in there could drive me so far. Theodore was ranting on about the hole in his arm from scaling the river bank. How it wasn't going to heal. He'd get gangrene. We'd have to cut it off. He'd go into shock and die and then we'd eat his body." Roger kept his eyes on the ceiling. "That was a seed and it grew faster than any weed on this planet. I knew it was a ripe opportunity."

I looked to O'Kief in disbelief. I could see Roger out of the corner of my eye and half expected him to jump on me and tear flesh with the last of his shattered teeth. My body shivered like an icicle in the warming daylight. O'Kief was bug-eyed with bags from fresh tormented sleep.

"Then this daydreaming, this fantasizing. It's too much."

"Go back," I said. "Finish with Theodore."

Roger looked at me and threw his stare back onto the ceiling. "I knew we'd die in here without food. It was clear from jump that this wasn't passing over quickly. I put the lie into my heart that I could tell you all Teddy was bit by a snake deep into the tunnel almost to the river bank. That I couldn't see it, that he yelled, "Snake," must have spooked it and it bit him and tore ass to the daylight. I would come back and we'd all agree that we shouldn't waste the meat. I'd volunteer to do the dirty work of taking the body through to the river and carving up the meat." He shot a look at Ipsic, who was still asleep at the far end of the cabin. "But that mother fucker and his paranoid selfishness came up with the notion that if Teddy was poisoned and died then we would die too if we ate his poisoned carcass. Through all the arguing of whether or not to eat the bastard I couldn't come clean and say I killed him in a moment of weakness. That his body was theoretically clean. I mean you remember the stories," Roger chuckled a little madman laugh, "how much he got laid. How many times he said he contracted minor VD. Just don't eat the wiener right?"

I could only imagine the look on O'Kief's face was as twisted as mine at Roger's display of disassociation from his crime.

END

THE DEATH OF MARCUS KASPAROV

　　　　The earth swallowed Marcus Kasparov in a
monumental yawn.
　　　　Gambel Oak and Alder, Cottonwood and Maple
stood with the slightest of movement. Scattered and alone,
they heaved the heavy sigh of widows whenever a gust of
wind shot through the air on its ceaseless search for
whatever it is that the wind may dream for. Pillars of

severity, they stood watch but for what they knew not. In every region they've been sung about and used in poetry by men and women constructing mirrors of their humanity with the natural tools around them; sky, birds, rain, reptiles, and trees.

In this place, the trees had a larger duty; to keep the living. The departed abound, fretless upon the air though their bones may be interred; the living need to be kept from chasing after them, from losing themselves in the thoughts of perilous infinity.

From the black.

These Gambel Oak and Alder, Cottonwood and Maple are anchors by which the living may be tethered; to draw down sad eyes from the limitless sky should they search for the reason and sense…should they seek the quiet infinitude of their longing to build wings to fly toward despair.

Marcus Kasparov was lowered into the ground on a sunny morning in a depressing September. The Catholic priest quietly cursed the man as blessings spilled out of his mouth in a dutiful performance for the three children of Kasparov; one daughter, Polly, and two sons, Ogden and Aleksandr. The three stood at the side of their father's grave. The elder son, Aleksandr, stood with the produce of overactive saliva glands in his mouth—he swallowed it and his pride and waited. His brother Ogden, was shaking in his wingtips, so Aleksandr held his composure and thought of things to repair on his motorcycle before he left town. Polly was dropping infrequent tears upon her lap as her head got lighter and lighter by the entrancing bereavement. The sadness filled her with half-questions that grew out of each other, one coming too quickly on the heels of the other to allow it to be thought. The death questions mingled with nonsense ("Did I leave the oven on? Did I lock the front door? What did I eat for dinner last night?").

Father Domingo ended the service and offered his sympathy to the three children of Kasparov. He walked to his car and removed the funeral vestments which he hung on a hanger in his back seat. He gave one last look to the gravesite and saw Aleksandr, Ogden, and Polly walking away from their father's grave. Father Domingo got into his Town Car and left the cemetery, one of only two in Bagdad, Arizona. About eighty-five percent of all burials were at that Catholic cemetery; "All others please use other door", a sign should have read at the gate to instruct nonbelievers on how to enter heaven.

"I don't know if I'm ready for this." Polly said.

"Ready for what?" Ogden said.

"Life without dad." she said.

"I don't think any of us are." Ogden said.

Aleksandr remained silent as they approached their vehicles. He had very little sympathy for Marcus but was not going to aggravate his brother and sister with his own personal feelings.

Polly said, "Hey, guys…I'm going to go back to my motel room. I don't think I can go back to dad's house right now, you know."

"You sure, sis?" Ogden said.

"Yeah. Could you guys clean up his kitchen today? I'm sorry. I just couldn't be there…knowing." she said.

"I'll take care of it, Polly. Get some rest and we can meet up later, get some dinner or something." Ogden said.

"Thanks, both of you." she said. She hugged them both and left the cemetery in her rental car.

The two brothers stood at the curb, on the fresh cut grass, exposed in the sun, and in thoughts as far away from the other's as Tokyo is from Rome. Only Ogden was actually thinking of the recently departed man who was once father to them both. Aleksandr stared desperately into the distance as though he might pull himself into the open desert; a blur of highway exit signs passed through his mind.

"Are you still coming back to dad's house with me?" Ogden said.

"For a little bit."

"I'll see you there, then." Ogden said and opened his car door. He watched Aleksandr jump down on his starter and sit for a moment twisting the handle bar. Aleksandr, with sunglasses masking his hate, made a point to look out, away from their father's gravesite. He rode out of the cemetery's winding lane with a haste of mind that urged him to just cut across the graves and make a quicker exit. He controlled the impulse and got out onto Lincoln and rode to their father's house.

Ogden started his car and sat for a moment. He turned the radio off and looked toward his father's plot. Tears came down over blood-warm cheeks like slow wine builds toward the face. His holy weeping was the full sadness of every service, every body interred at that cemetery. Every word, each step, and congratulatory handshake his father made in his presence was an affirmation of Ogden's own worth, and value, and pride.

The leaves above his windshield shimmered in the sunlight and were a million condolences. A curious squirrel clung with purposeful claws to the trunk of an elm and surveyed the stone bespeckled lawn. Ogden calmed when it sunk in, in a very abstract, intangible way, that this is life. He seemed to understand the plot—timelines, communication of experience, the passing down of knowledge, the insatiable questioning madness to understand some infinite puzzle (just under the surface of it all—so easy you wouldn't believe it—"Where are the keys?"—"In the door."—"Have you seen my glasses?"—"On top of your head.")

Ogden put his car in drive. Tears blurred his eyes; he didn't want to wipe them away because they were truth. His front, right tire bumped a curbstone and the present came to him in judgment and placed the infinite truth in contempt. He wiped away the tears and drove to his father's home to meet Aleksandr.

Ogden walked into the living room of his father's house and found Aleksandr examining a photograph of

Maria, Ogden's mother, in a glass frame. "Sorry about your mom, bro." Aleksandr said. "She died pretty unexpectedly."

"Thanks."

"Can you believe mo- …Emma died so young too?" Aleksandr said.

"No. I'd like to have known your mom. But, I guess you didn't get a chance to know her either. Sorry about that." Ogden said.

"Kinda makes you wonder, don't it?"

"'Bout what?"

"Why the women in dad's life gave birth and then died not long after." Aleksandr said.

"In his defense, my Mom died when I was almost fourteen." Ogden said.

"Good point. Well, not good, but you know what I mean." Aleksandr put the picture of Ogden's mother down on the bookshelf.

"I know what you mean."

The house was still 'alive' but the feeling wouldn't live out the week.

"So, little brother, I'm having some of the scotch, do you want one?" Aleksandr said. "Too early?"

"No, I don't drink scotch. Is there gin? I'll fix mine." Ogden said as he walked to the kitchen.

"Yep. The old man's got some gin. Had, some gin."

The two brothers stood at opposite ends of the long kitchen counter fixing their own drinks. For Aleksandr, this amounted to sloshing three fingers into a little glass and setting the bottle down without replacing the cap. "What do you do again, in New York City?" he said. He attempted a sincere interest in Ogden's life because deep down he didn't want his brother to think he hated him, and he didn't—he just came off that way.

"I write with other writers for the Jones Show and American Truth with Harvey Mitberg." Ogden was savoring the slicing of the lime wedge for the G&T he poured with all the aplomb of a mad scientist on the verge of a breakthrough.

"Write? I thought you did geek stuff in the control room? You didn't go to school for writing." Aleksandr said, two fingers down on his scotch.

"Actually, I did, for journalism at Columbia. Remember?" Ogden gave the wedge a little squeeze over his G&T and the lime juice fell like bombs over the icy surface of his drink.

"Right, journalism."

"Of course, what we do on our shows, especially The Jones Show, is pretty goddamn far from journalism."

"How's that?" Aleksandr lit a cigarette in the kitchen. Ogden looked at him sideways as he was about to speak.

"If we did The Jones shit at a live theater we could get busted every time for inciting a riot." Ogden said. Aleksandr held out his smokes to Ogden. "No, thanks." Ogden's eyes darted around the room.

"Don't worry. I won't tell the old man you smoked in his house."

"I quit a while ago, Aleks."

"You're in the news business and you don't smoke? I can't believe they haven't eaten you alive yet."

"It's a new business, man. But, I'll have one here." Ogden grabbed a smoke and Aleksandr's lighter and lit up, there in his father's kitchen. He exhaled and the smoke weaved through the lost possessions of the dead man's past. The smoke hung in the air among the copper pots and kettles that hung on the walls, among the framed black and white photos Marcus had taken out in the desert, and among the few dirty dishes he'd been cleaning when the heart attack dropped him.

What goes through your mind when you're dying in the middle of the dishes? How many loads of dishes do you do at home before it becomes something other than a chore, before you stop wishing you had a maid, before you start to enjoy this one "little thing" in life?

They shared Aleksandr's cigarettes and drank their drinks. Among the framed black and white photos Marcus had taken on a trip once to the Coconino Plateau west of Painted Desert in the heat of a terrifying Arizona summer back in the 1970's.

"Do you like Pocatello?" Ogden said. "You've been there how long?"

"A few years. It's got its good and bad, like anywhere that has streets and water treatment facilities. I don't know what side you'd place me on in that good/bad axis but the job at Frank's Motorcycles is good." Aleksandr splashed out a third, three finger glass of scotch and lit a cigarette out of a fresh pack. "You guys doing much on the Africa wars?"

"Every other night, Jones has an eight minute rant on the pros and cons, mostly pros, of the wars on the continent."

"Eight minutes, shit. I guess the world still doesn't give two shits about the people over there. Those refugees could take Europe barehanded. They got the numbers."

"Eight minutes is more than most places have gotten on shows like ours over the past twenty years."

"So, you basically write bullshit that comes out of another man's mouth?"

"Yeah, and I'm one of the best." Ogden said. He bombed his third little arctic village of G&T with another sortie of lime juice. "Those 'refugees', by the way, are the bastard war lords and juntas that oppressed all those tribes for so long they're finally getting their own shit handed back to them. I know I don't feel bad that an oppressed continent is rising up and asserting itself against the power blind militias that never hesitated to exploit their brothers and sisters from the womb to the grave, or should I say, the mass grave."

"Right on, Ogden. I don't spend too much time thinking about that shit. I'm too busy fighting and fucking to map out the world's sorrows. Got my own, you know?"

"I know what you mean. That shit's my job though. Kinda lucky, because all the politics is interesting as hell to me, older brother." Ogden tilted his drink toward Aleksandr and raised his glass, "To the old man." he said.

Aleksandr raised his glass and nodded his head, 'Fuck him.' he thought to himself.

At an empty biker bar on the outskirts of Hurricane, Utah, Polly's husband Daniel was pacing the parking lot in a calm and concerned way. "How long are you going to stay in Bagdad?" he said.

On the other end of the phone, Polly said, "I think I'll be here one more hot day. This whole town feels empty and wrong now."

"Do you want me to come out there?"

"No, go ahead and keep the bar open. I'll be okay after a while…I want to talk to him again…hear his voice." she said.

"I'm sorry, Polly."

"It's alright. Uh. Did you get the license renewed?"

"Yeah. Don't worry about that. How are your brothers?" Daniel said.

"I don't know. Ogden seems pretty broken up. I think he's sad he's been so far away for the past years."

"Yeah? What about Aleks?"

"You know, we've got a lot in common with Aleksandr, you and I, but I think sometimes he's got a heart of stone. He doesn't seem bothered that dad's gone."

"Could be in shock."

"Doubt it. I don't think he ever stopped blaming dad for Emma's death. And who really knows if he should?" Polly said.

"I guess it's something he's going to have to figure out for himself."

"I know."

A half dozen men on motorcycles thundered into the parking lot where Daniel stood. "Well babe, we got customers. Are you sure you'll be alright?"

"Yeah. I'll see you in a couple of days. I'll call you tomorrow though."

"I love you." he said.

"I love you too, Daniel." she said.

Ogden and Aleksandr had finished cleaning up Marcus' kitchen. They were sitting outside on the patio that looked out onto the expanse of the old man's ranch. It looked like Mars out there where the land sloped down to the horizon. From where they sat, the land went out for fifty yards, dropped off, and didn't seem to rise up again for miles. They'd taken the gin and scotch out with them and were slowly draining their bottles.

"This is such a beautiful ranch dad had here. He loved to come out here on the deck and watch the sunsets. He said he felt that each day drew to a close out here like grand theater with the night dropping like a slow curtain on the southwest." Aleksandr grunted agreement. Ogden went on, "Did you hate my mom when you were living with us, Aleksandr?"

"No, I didn't hate Maria. I probably made everyone think that but I've been so pissed at dad since my mom died…"

"Yeah. I just always wondered if maybe Maria had done something to piss you off. I understand though, what you're saying." Ogden said.

Aleksandr looked out off the patio deck but in his mind he was looking at his brother, yelling at him that he didn't understand the first thing about it. He turned to look at Ogden, "I still blame that bastard for Emma's death. I was seven years old but I knew what happened. He shouldn't have been riding out there at that mine with her like that. She died from his carelessness and…just plain fucking stupidity. You wanna go defy death, do it on your own. Don't put someone else's life in danger too just because you think you're immortal. That's why I still hate him."

Ogden remained silent for a while, wiping the sweat from his glass with his thumb as he leaned on a railing that wrapped around the deck. He tried to think of something to say to reassure his brother…to defend his father…to make amends on behalf of Marcus' soul. Thoughts ran so chaotic in his mind that they cancelled themselves out and his brain seemed to be silent except for registering the wind, the beat of his own heart intensified by the alcohol and cigarettes, and the reaper's scream coming from the throats of ravenous vultures that circled above fresh meat out there in the western expanse of Marcus Kasparov's sprawling ranch.

Bury your dead.

END

THE NEWS ON TV

The Stranger　　　　　March 4

Clerk Slain
In Early Morning Hold Up
Story by Kim Bensin

Twin Valley - Police responded to an anonymous call from a payphone outside of the ExpediMart of a robbery in progress. When officers arrived on the scene, only moments later, they found the clerk shot three times lying behind the counter.

The clerk, identified as Mark Epstine, had been working as the graveyard shift cashier for only two and a half weeks, the manager said. "Tragic, tragic. An accident like this will make it hard to keep our doors open. We'll see, in the days to come, what choice will be appropriate to make." the manager indicated further that Mr. Epstine had taken the job to pay for an ailing child's medical bills.

Area residents were in shock. Though there has been a rash of armed hold ups in the past few weeks across the city, the well-manicured neighborhood had been free of violent crime for nearly three years.

"All of a sudden, it's like your piece of mind is shattered," said one neighborhood resident. Betsy Attelscraft continued, saying,

"I've lived in this area since most of the town was destroyed by the tornado and this is the sickest thing I've heard of happening here."

At this time, police are analyzing the security footage for further detail of the assailant's features but as of now, they say the suspect was in a bright orange track suit, wearing a Twin Valley baseball cap marked with the TV logo.

The victim's parents have set up a memorial fund to ensure the continued medical treatment for Mr. Epstine's child. Contributions may be made at any Landon State Bank branch.

Inside of the ExpediMart when it was dark outside you could see about three feet into the parking lot. The rest was just a reflection of the bright consumer hodgepodge spread out within. It was a large venue for snack foods and refreshments, condiments and cigarettes, and all the random paraphernalia found in kitchen junk drawers across the country.

The door came open and a young guy walked in. From behind the counter, at a distance of twenty-five feet, Mark could tell the boy was probably just a senior in high school. The kid nodded once with an overtly aggressive knock back of his head. Mark thought he also pursed his lip, not intentionally trying to look like Elvis Presly but coming off that way anyway. It was early in the morning. Or, late in the night. Either way, too late to give a shit about acting cool. 'Ah damn these bills. Goddamn this sickness,' Mark thought and drummed his fingertips on top of the clear acrylic lottery ticket case.

"Hey bud," the kid said.

"Late night?"

"Always, my man."

'Wow, this guy is cool. No wonder he's here alone.' Mark watched the kid mill around the beer coolers for a few minutes, checking back over his shoulder to see if Mark was watching him. When the kid caught his eye he sniggered and walked up the aisle where the coffee machines stood.

Mark flipped through the The Stranger, looking for the classifieds to see if there were any better part time jobs out there than his crappy clerk position at the ExpediMart. He rustled the paper to remind the kid that he wasn't alone in there. The kid made a coffee, which seemed to Mark to take an extra-ordinary amount of time and concentration on the part of the kid. He came up to the counter stirring the drink feverishly with a regular straw. "Uh, buck sixty-five for the coffee?"

"Sorry, new here. Have to ring it up to see."

"Thought you were." The kid blew on his drink. "I'm Josh. My old man lives up the hill, round the corner."

"Josh, I'm Mark." The machine sprang alive with a quick humming of activity, electro-radiating through the slits of hard plastic vents. "So, it's none of my business and I don't really care otherwise but you look like you'd still be in high school?"

"Sure. What about it, Mark?"

"Just, pretty late."

"Yeah. Or early, who's to say? Don't worry though. My old man's outta town a lot so I spend a good amount of time taking care of myself. I like to come down here and catch the paper when it's fresh off the truck."

"I see. Well, that's pretty noble of you."

"Not really. Can I get a pack of Red Dogs?" Josh dug the cash out of his coat pocket and they made the transaction. "It'd be nobler, I think, if The Stranger hadn't become such a shit paper."

"How do you mean?"

"Think about what you pay your couple a quarters for man, when it's all said and done. When you read everything you wanted to read, what's left? Not enough quality paper to wipe with."

"How long have you been reading this paper? You got a pretty strong opinion of it, at eighteen?"

"My mom and I used to sit down and read it together when I was five. Every morning, she'd sit me on her knee, with her cup of coffee and a bowl of oatmeal for me beside the daily edition of The Stranger." Josh took the plastic straw from the coffee and took a sip. He stirred it again, "Still too hot. Do they keep that coffee maker on Super Fucking Nuclear Hot?"

"You're asking the wrong guy."

"So what's your story?"

"Need the money."

"Everybody does. Most people don't take a graveyard shift at a gas station though to make up for it."

"Do you pry this much into everybody's lives?"

"Too short not to care, even if you have to fake it, right?"

"Enjoy your paper."

"Not since the new editor took it over six years ago," Josh said and took a seat at one of the booths that lined the wall of windows at the front of the ExpediMart.

The bell over the door rang and a tall, svelte woman in a black trench with red hair pulled behind swept bangs into a pony tail walked in; quick, brisk steps on pointed heels to the register. Mark nodded with a shy smile and felt a twinge of guilt at the instant attraction to her. But it was fleeting and he knew it and knew his soul was not so tarnished.

"Huuuuh," she exhaled and a bit of frost blew out from between her roseate lips. "I can't get my card to work out at the pump."

"I can take care of that for you. They said they were having problems with that card reader."

"Yeah well, maybe they should put up a sign so people who have to be somewhere don't have to waste their time."

"'Mm sorry for the trouble."

"I'm sorry. It's early," she said.

"Or late?" Mark suggested.

"Perhaps."

"Take care miss."

"Thanks," she said and made her way to the door passing Josh walking to the counter.

"And with that she slid out of his fingertips forever. As a mist upon the lake."

"Quite a poetic statement from a young tough like you. But," Mark held up his hand, "I'm married."

"Aren't we all, to the stunning female form."

"Yeah yeah yeah."

"I wanted to show you what I meant," Josh unrolled the paper across the counter. "About the editor?"

"Oh. Right. What's the deal?"

"See here, in this article. Can you tell me, what's the point? The theme? The overall tone is tacitly juvenile also. This is supposed to be a professional journalistic endeavour but he's diminished it. Tarnished it, actually ground it down to a base more corrupt than the old yellow journalism of the late 19th century."

"Wow. That your thesis?"

"What?"

"No, I'm just saying, it's kinda late to be worrying about this kinda thing."

"Or early."

"That too. Sorry, I'm just a little wiped working this second job."

The bell above the door rang. Mark noted the TV ball cap, after the bright orange track suit. And, after the green handgun.

END